The Princess of the Chalet School

This Armada book belongs to:

_____

_____

_____

The Chalet School series by Elinor M. Brent-Dyer

This is a complete list of Chalet School titles in chronological order. Those title printed in bold type have been published in paperback in Armada but not all are currently available.

Elinor M. Brent-Dyer

The Princess of
the Chalet School

Armada

The Princess of the Chalet School was first published in
the U.K. by W. & R. Chambers Ltd, London & Edinburgh
This edition was first published in Armada in 1968
This impression 1990

Armada is an imprint of
the Children's Division, part of
Harper Collins Publishers,
8 Grafton Street, London W1X 3LA

Printed and bound in Great Britain by
William Collins Sons & Co. Ltd, Glasgow

CHAPTER I

A WEARY PATIENT

INTO the pretty bedroom came the great English doctor, a jolly smile on his face as he approached the bed where his patient was lying. "Good-morning, your Highness. How are you this morning?" he cried.

The little girl on the bed looked at him wearily. "I am getting better, thank you," she replied in listless tones which made the doctor frown.

The younger man who had entered the room with him bent over the child. "Still rather tired, my darling?" he asked tenderly.

"Just a little, daddy."

"It's the dreadful weather," he said, looking out of the window at the rain which poured steadily down. "When it's fine again, you'll soon be all right."

"Shall I?" Her Royal Highness the Princess Elisaveta Margherita of Belsornia looked at her father with a little wondering smile.

"Why, yes! That is what good Dr Tracy says."

The doctor nodded as the great dark eyes were turned on him. "Yes, indeed, Highness. It is true. And how would you like to get up for a while this afternoon?"

The Princess shook her head. "I'm so tired," she said. "I don't think I shall ever want to get up again."

"Nonsense!" declared the physician. "You shall get up for a short while, and I expect you will soon be making an outcry if I suggest keeping you in bed an hour longer than need be." He made a short examination of her, and then stood back, still frowning slightly.

The Crown Prince of Belsornia glanced at him. "Will that be all at present, sir?" he asked in his pleasant voice.

"All I want just now, thank you," replied the doctor. "I will come in this afternoon, after her Highness has got up, and see how she feels." He smiled at the little girl. "I am sure she will feel much better soon."

He stepped back from the bed, and the Crown Prince took his place. "I must leave you now, Carina. There is a meeting of the Grand Council, and they need me. I will try to come and have tea with you this afternoon though, so you must be sitting up, ready to pour it out for me."

Elisaveta nodded. "Yes; I will. You *will* come, daddy?"

"If it's at all possible. If the welfare of the kingdom doesn't require my immediate attention! You'll be good, old lady, and eat all your luncheon?"

"Yes, daddy. At least, I'll *try*," promised the Princess. "I do hope the kingdom won't need you. It's so lonely by myself!"

"Oh, come! You have Nurse, and Alette, to say nothing of Mademoiselle!"

"I know; but they don't play as you do. So you'll come, daddy? And you come, too, doctor," she added politely.

"Perhaps," laughed the doctor. "If I am not wanted at the hospital I will come with pleasure."

They said good-bye to her, and then they went out of the room, the Crown Prince turning back to throw kisses to her as she lay on her big pillows. Once they were out of hearing, however, he caught the doctor by the arm. "Tracy, come into my library a minute. I must know what you think of Elisaveta! I am horribly worried about her—she seems so listless and weak. She always was such a jolly kiddy; it isn't at all like her to be so languid."

They entered the great library as he finished speaking, and sat down beside the blazing wood fire. The doctor looked at the Prince for a moment before he replied. "It would not be fair to you, Prince, to hide from you that I *am* anxious about the Princess's slow recovery," he said at length. "Of course, bronchial influenza is a nasty thing, and the Princess has had a sharp attack; still, she ought to be picking up, now. The worrying thing is that she is making little or no headway. I think she needs rousing. That is why I am so determined that she shall get up, if only for a short while this afternoon. I was thankful that you backed me up in it."

"Well, I could do no less. But tell me, Tracy, is there anything I can do to help matters on? I'll do anything I can."

"So far as I can see, the only thing you could do would be to give up your position as Crown Prince and settle down as an ordinary man," said the doctor dryly. "Her

6

Royal Highness is suffering mainly from lack of suitable companions, and you are the only one she can have—and she gets very little of you."

The Prince threw out his hands with a gesture of despair. "That's all very well, but what can I do? I'd willingly give up my claim to the throne, but my father would never hear of it, and you know that in Belsornia the heir cannot give up his rights without the consent of the King and the Government. The next after me is my cousin, Cosimo, and he is not exactly the type of heir of whom one can be proud!"

"He isn't," agreed the doctor, his mind going to some of the escapades which had made Prince Cosimo one of the most hated royalties on the Continent.

"Well, then, suggest something possible."

The doctor thought again. "There can never be any question of Princess Elisaveta succeeding to the throne?" he queried.

"None. The Salic law holds good here. I believe the Belsorians would rather become a republic than have a woman on the throne!"

"Then why not send her to school?"

The Prince raised his eyebrows. "To school? I don't know what the King would say to that. It's never been done in our family—not for the girls. Of course, I had a year at Eton and two at Oxford. But that was only thanks to my mother. She was English, you know, and she persuaded my father to agree to it. But for a girl, I don't know if he would consent. Where would you suggest sending her?"

"Not to England! I love my country, but not her climate, and the English winters with the heavy fogs would be the last thing for the Princess. No; what I have in mind is something far better than that. I have a friend who has just sent his daughter to a school in the Austrian Tyrol. It is quite a big school, I am told, run by an English girl. It is up in the mountains, beside the Tiern See, and is just the very thing we need—if his Majesty will give his consent."

"The Tiern See? I went there once—when I was on my honeymoon. I remember it well. It was very beautiful and ringed round with mountains. So there is a school there now? A good school?"

"Very! I am sure of that, or my friend would never have sent his child there. She is an only child—and motherless."

"Like my poor little Elisaveta. I believe you are right,

Tracy. If she had companions, I think she would soon be all right."

"I am sure of it," said the physician with conviction. Then he suddenly let himself go: "For heaven's sake, Prince, can't you see that all the court ceremony and restrictions are simply sucking the child's vitality away? She has no chance to be child-like. What has a baby of twelve to do with 'the welfare of the kingdom'? She ought to be climbing trees, and sliding down the bannisters; not troubling herself with the meetings of the Grand Council! I'd rather see the Princess black with mud and wearing a badly torn frock, than in her prettiest robes and helping to receive royalty like a young queen. The one's natural childhood— the other isn't!"

"I agree," said her father. "You are right. If words can do it, my father shall consent to it to-night. After all, the child is mine. She shall not die for lack of what the poorest child in the kingdom has. If he won't agree, she shall be smuggled out of the country somehow! There's my hand on it!"

He held out his hand, and the doctor gripped it. "I wish you success with his Majesty with all my heart, Prince. I think perhaps he may agree."

Then the two men went on their way, the Prince to a meeting of the Grand Council, where he was to represent his father, and the doctor to the children's hospital, where he was doing such grand work for Belsornia.

In the meantime, the Princess, never dreaming of what was to happen, had fallen into her favourite day-dream, and was arriving at school, where there were lots of nice girls who were all anxious to be friendly and work and play with her, as she had read of girls doing in the school-stories which her father had given her. One of Elisaveta's chief reasons for not getting well too quickly was that when she was well there was too little time for dreaming. There were lessons with her three governesses, who were all deeply concerned in turning out Elisaveta as a credit to her family. The Belsornian princesses had always been renowned for their learning, and it seemed to the three ladies who had charge of the latest princess, that she must not fall short of the standard set by her ancestresses. So Mademoiselle de Séguiné insisted on a great deal of French, literature, and astronomy; Signorino di Basaco taught history of the world, Italian, Latin, and Greek; Miss Bruce was very thorough over all mathematics and chemistry. Botany was taught by one of the professors from the Firarto University; and German and music were in the charge of an old Bavarian, who came to the place twice a week for his subjects. Much reading of those delightful stories which were kept in the book-case in her sitting-room was forbidden, and Princess Elisaveta led a strenuous life when she was well. Since she had begun to get better after her sharp illness, she had begun to feel a dread of the return of the old schoolroom days. It seemed to her that she *could* not go back to the long lesson hours and the dull days when she saw her father for few minutes only.

When three o'clock brought Alette, her maid, to dress her ready to be carried to the big arm-chair by the fire, she felt ready to cry. However, her training held good, and she allowed Alette to put her into her pale blue velvet dressing-gown with the slippers to match, and wrap a white shawl of embroidered Indian silk round her, without making any remarks. After that the nurse carried her across the room and settled her comfortably in the big arm-chair, in which she could almost lie at full length. The tea-table was arranged, and then Mademoiselle, who had left her to Nurse and Alette lately, made her appearance. "This is better, my dear Elisaveta," she remarked as she sat down. "Now, if you will only make a little effort, I am sure you will soon be quite all right again. We shall have to work very hard, once you are back in the schoolroom, you know, to make up all you have lost during your illness. I hope you have not forgotten everything."

This was not very cheering conversation for the invalid, and Elisaveta simply sat silent, though she was making up her mind that she would not go near the schoolroom till she absolutely had to. She glanced at the clock. Surely her father was very late. He should have been with her quite ten minutes ago. Suppose he could not come!

Mademoiselle saw where her look went, and guessed the cause of it. "It is only ten minutes after the time, yet," she said kindly. "His Highness would certainly have sent a message if he had been prevented from coming."

Before Elisaveta could answer her, there was the sound of quick, light steps along the corridor, and then the door opened, and daddy came in.

Mademoiselle rose at once, of course. She curtseyed to

9

the Prince. "Have I your permission to retire, sire?" she murmured.

"Thank you, Mademoiselle." replied daddy. "I will look after this bad child for a while. You must need a holiday."

"Thank you, sire," replied Mademoiselle; "but Elisaveta is a good child on the whole, and I am glad she shows signs of improvement." Then she curtseyed again and left the room, while Elisaveta sat literally dumb with surprise at the first part of her speech. She had not known that she was good at all, much less that Mademoiselle thought so!

CHAPTER II

THE NEW PLAN

AS soon as Mademoiselle had left the room Elisaveta turned to her father eagerly. "Daddy! What an extraordinary thing for her to say! She *never* praises me!"

She spoke in the English her father loved for the sake of his long-dead mother, and which they always used when they were alone together. The thought now crossed his mind that it was as well, since she was to go to an English school. "I expect she wants to encourage you to hurry up and get well," he told his little daughter, laughing.

Elisaveta sighed deeply. "I don't think I want to get well, daddy. I'd rather remain as I am."

"Why?" he asked quietly.

There was a moment's silence. Then out it all came—the whole of the loneliness and unhappiness that she had managed to suppress up to date. "Daddy! It's so lonely, all by myself! They all mean to be kind, but they don't know how to play, and they think I'm too big, anyway. I don't want to be learned or discover stars, or make wonderful translations from the Greek—or anything like that! I only want to do the things other girls do! Oh, daddy! I want to go to school!"

It was out—the secret longing of which she had never spoken to a single person until this moment. Now she had spoken it she suddenly wished she hadn't. It seemed so silly, and it was so impossible. The princesses of Belsornia never went to schools.

The Crown Prince did not answer his little daughter's outburst immediately, and she began to be afraid that he minded her wanting to go away. She peeped at him from under her long lashes, and then she discovered that he was smiling. "Daddy!" she cried, a sudden wonderful idea in her head.

"Well, what?" he asked.

"Do you—am I—is it——"

"What a number of unfinished sentences!" he laughed, as he took her hands in his. "And so that is your dream—to go to school?"

Elisaveta nodded dumbly; she was incapable of speaking at the moment.

"Would it make you very happy to go, Carina?"

Again the little nod of the head.

"Then you shall. I am going to send Signor Francesco to the Tiern See, where there is a good school, kept by an English lady, and he will make all arrangements for you to go there after Easter. Does it please you, my darling?"

"Grandpapa?" breathed Elisaveta.

"He agrees. He thinks with me that you will be happier with other girls, and the school is a good one, with the highest testimonials—so he has consented. Alette must see to getting your clothes ready, and I think we will give *les gouvernantes* a little holiday. You won't want to do lessons for the next few weeks, will you?"

"Oh! It's too good to be true!" Elisaveta was squeezing her father's hands so tightly in her excitement that he was surprised. "Daddy, it's ever so good of grandpapa! I was so afraid that he would mind. All the girls of our family have just had governesses, and I thought he would say that I must, too. It is splendid that he doesn't! I suppose he's a very enlightened monarch!"

The last sentence of that speech would have decided her father if nothing else had done so. It was so utterly unchildlike. However, he said nothing about it, and Elisaveta was too much interested in her future to worry much about her grandfather, who had never shown much interest in her, the truth being that he had never really forgiven her for not being a boy.

"What do we wear, daddy? Will it be gym tunics, like

11

the girls in the books you give me? I do hope so! It must be so lovely to wear frocks that don't really matter! "

"Don't you like pretty frocks?" asked her father curiously.

"Sometimes—when I come to a reception, or anything of that kind. But it's just hateful to have to be careful of all my frocks!"

"Well, I expect you will wear a tunic, so you needn't worry about that any longer," said the Prince, laughing. "Here comes Alette with the tea. Will you pour out, yourself?"

"I'll pour out," decided the Princess. "You must just be my visitor, daddy."

She carefully poured out his tea, and saw him supplied with muffin from the dish Alette had brought into the room with the tea. Then she went back to the school. "Tell me all about it, daddy, *please!*"

"I really can't tell you very much yet. I only know what the doctor told me. It is built on the shores of the Tiern See, where your mother and I spent part of our honeymoon. It is kept by an English girl—a Miss Bettany. She has a French lady for partner, I believe, and she receives girls who want an English education. Dr Tracy tells me that a friend of his just sent his little girl there, so I hope she will be a friend for you. That is all I know about it. I have told Captain Trevillion to write for the prospectus, and we'll know more about it when that comes. Aren't you going to eat anything?"

"I forgot," acknowledged the Princess, who, in her excitement, had taken nothing so far. "I think I'd like some of that spongecake, daddy, please."

He passed it to her, and while she ate it her thoughts went back to her grandfather. "It seems so strange that I can really go," she said. "I was sure that grandpapa would always say 'No,' so I never said anything about it. Are you *certain* he doesn't mind, daddy?"

"Certain. So you needn't think of that any more. Only don't talk too much about it before him," replied the Prince, his mind going back to the interview he had had with his father half an hour ago.

"I don't approve of schools for girls," the King had said. "Still, as you have reminded me, she is your child, so you have a right to dispose of her as you choose, I suppose. She is a girl—can never wear the crown—so I do not think it

12

can matter much what you do with her. Send her, by all means, if you feel that it is your duty—I shall not forbid it. If she had been a boy it would have been different. As it is, I have to look forward to the fact that after you comes Cosimo. I wish you would marry again, Carol."

The Crown Prince shook his head. "I regret, sire, I cannot do that. And Cosimo may yet reform."

"Never!" reported the King. "Well, if you refuse, I cannot force you; I can only point you to your duty to the realm. But with regard to Elisaveta you may do as you please. She will never come to the throne, and we are only a very negligible kingdom now. It can make no difference to us when she is of marriageable age."

"Thank you sire." The Prince rose. "I am deeply grateful to you for your consent, and if I could do anything to thank you, I would do it. But what you have asked is more than I can do."

The King bent his head. "So be it. Yet I may ask again, Carol. Yet I will not press you."

Prince Carol looked at his father. Then greatly daring, he spoke once more before leaving the room. "Your Majesty will be the last one to press such a thing on me, even for the good of the realm. I remember my mother."

Then he had left the room to bring the glad news to his little daughter, leaving his father thinking of the lovely English wife who had taken most of the sunlight from his life when she died. The Crown Prince was right. The King would never force his son to remarry, and Elisaveta had no need at present, anyhow, to fear a step-mother. As a matter of fact, such an idea had never entered her head. She was very childish, and no one had ever hinted at such an idea to her. At least, she was very far from thinking of anything of the kind that rainy afternoon in February when she discussed so eagerly the question of her school with her father.

At about five o'clock by English time—seventeen, by continental measures—Dr Tracy made his appearance, and was literally startled by the change in his little patient. Gone was the listlessness of the morning, and a merry, flushed child greeted him with eager exclamations. "Oh, Dr Tracy, I am so glad to see you! I want to thank you for saying I ought to go to school. It was so kind of you, and to think of a school, too!"

"Kind, was it?" queried the doctor as he looked at her.

13

"Well, I don't know. I think it was the best thing to do when all my medicine and all Nurse's care weren't helping you to get well as quickly as you ought. You like this medicine, do you?"

"Oh, ever so much!" And the Princess held out her hand to him. "It is lovely, and I think you are a dear to have thought of it!"

"Good! Well, if you can look like this after only a short while of it, you ought soon to be out of my hands now. You must eat and sleep, and make haste to get well as soon as possible, for Alette will need you to make your new outfit, and I want to see you all ready for school before the end of next month."

"Does the term begin at the end of March?" asked Elisaveta, astonished.

"No; not till the beginning of May, I believe. But I want you to have a holiday first, and you must go to Elmiano for a few weeks before you make the long journey to the Tyrol."

"How lovely! I love Elmiano!!" sighed Elisaveta, who associated the lovely seaside village with summer holidays spent in getting herself into as much of a mess as possible, with only Alette to raise her hands in horror, and the Baroness Salnio, who was her lady-in-waiting, to say, "Oh, Princess, how you have dirtied yourself!"

"Then that's settled," said the doctor. "In three weeks' time you be ready for the little trip, and then it will be hey for school and dozens of girls!"

"Ooh!" The Princess sighed a deep sigh of rapture. "It is just gorgeous. I'm longing for it!"

"Excellent! Well, now we must have nurse and Alette to get you back to bed, and to sleep. You will be tired after all this excitement, and I don't want you to be poorly to-morrow as a result of all your joy to come."

"I'll go to bed, of course," replied the Princess, "but I'm sure I shall never be able to go to sleep. I shall just lie and think of it all."

"We'll see," said the doctor, who knew better than to upset her by contradicting her. "I'll ring for Alette, and then you must say 'Good-bye' to his Highness for a while. He shall come to say 'Good-night' when you are safe in bed."

Nurse and Alette were startled at the improvement in their little charge since they had last seen her. Nurse, especially, was surprised. "Well, Princess," she said, as she laid the little girl in bed and tucked her in, "getting up *has* done you good! You don't look like the same child!"

Alette, who had been Elisaveta's nurse until her small mistress had gone into the schoolroom, and who adored the Princess with her whole heart, was overjoyed. "You look more like my bambina," she said in her soft pretty Belsornian. "It rejoices my heart to see you so, madame."

"Dear Alette!" said the Princess, smiling at her.

Alette finished her work of tidying up the room, and the nurse made up the fire and saw that the night-light was in its place.

"I'm not *really* sleepy, Nurse," said Elisaveta pleadingly.

Nurse smiled. "Not yet; but I expect you soon will be. I will leave the light a little longer, however, and I will sit by the fire and finish my book. But you must not talk, madame; you must lie quietly if I do so."

"I will," promised the Princess.

Elisaveta lay very still and watched her, turning over in her mind all that she had been told and all the splendid time that was coming to her. It seemed too wonderful to be true. Then she knew that it was; for she was there already, and was assuring a quite serious headmistress that she never went on a lake with other girls unless they had an elephant in the boat.

It was just at this point, though she did not know it, that Nurse lit the night-light, and, switching off the electric-light, stole out of the room. Elisaveta was sound asleep.

CHAPTER III

AN HONOUR FOR THE CHALET SCHOOL

"JOEY—Joey!"

"Coming!" Joey Bettany swung herself down from the big tree in which she had been sitting, and raced across the grass towards the house where her elder sister, Madge, was standing waiting for her.

"Where on earth were you?" demanded the latter as her

small sister reached her side. "I've been looking all over for you."

"I was only in the chestnut-tree," explained Joey, holding out her hands in corroboration of her statement. "Why didn't you call before? I'd have shouted, and then you wouldn't have had to look for me."

"I thought you were practising," replied Madge. "How you do love to climb about Joey! You must have been a monkey in your last incarnation, I should think!"

The two sisters began to stroll down the path to the high gate in the withy fence which kept summer visitors from gazing in at the girls during school-hours, and acted as a deterent on girls who preferred to see what people outside were doing to getting on with their work. It had been built during the previous Easter to take the place of one which had been swept away by the flooding of the mountain stream that flowed into the lake from the great Tiernjoch, and helped to divide the triangle of Briesau where the Chalet School was situated. Herr Braun, the landlord of Miss Bettany, had had the fence erected again while she and the school were having holiday, and it was a good substantial affair now, with strong iron staves driven into the ground at frequent intervals for supports, and with a double interlacing of the withes.

The two Bettanys walked down to the gate, opened it, crossed the little bridge the kindly Tyrolean had put over the deep ditch he had dug to carry off water in case such a thing should happen again, and turned down the lake road in the direction of the Post Hotel, one of the largest there.

"Where are we going?" demanded Joey.

"To the Post. Herr Sneider is ill, and I am going to fetch the letters—if there are any."

"There ought to be one from India. Dick is awfully regular. He's a jolly decent brother that way," declared Joey. "Mollie isn't bad, either. Isn't it funny?" she went on; "we've got a sister-in-law—had her more than a year, and neither of us has seen her. At least, you can't count photos really, can you?"

"It isn't quite the same thing," acknowledged Madge.

"What's wrong with Herr Sneider?" asked Jo.

"He got wet in the storm two days ago, and he's gone down with an attack of pleurisy. Everyone will have to fetch letters just now, I'm afraid, until he's better."

"Hard lines on the people who live right up the valley! It means a walk then!"

"There aren't very many letters that way during this part of the year," said Madge. "Here we are. Run along in and ask if there are any for us."

Jo vanished up the steps of the hotel to the room that was dignified by the name of post-office, and presently returned with a handful of letters and post-cards, which she gave to her sister. "See if there's one from India," she coaxed.

Madge shook her head. "Look at that sky! It's going to be another downpour. We must fly if we don't want to get wet. Come along!"

She tucked the letters into her pockets and the two went racing home at top-speed, for neither of them had hats, and Joey was only in her blazer. They reached the door just as the first drops began to fall, and turned into the study, where Madge sent her sister to change her shoes. Joey had been exceptionally delicate up to two years ago, when they had come from England to the Tyrol to start the school which had prospered so amazingly, and even now, when she was far stronger than they had ever thought possible, colds were things to be avoided in her case, though they were no longer the bugbears they had once been. She had heaps of spirit, but she would never be robust, and Madge still suffered agonies of anxiety about her from time to time.

She hurried back, to find her sister sorting out the letters at express speed.

"Here you are," she said, giving one bundle to the child. "Put those on the table, and then you can come back—there's a letter from India."

Jo vanished with the letters, which she hastily spread out on the table in the *Speisesaal,* and then returned to the study. "The others will get wet," she said, as she glanced out of the window. "It's literally emptying down. What's Dick say? Is there one from Mollie?"

"Give me time," laughed Madge. "I haven't opened it yet!" She slit open the envelope as she spoke and drew out the letter.

"There isn't" said Jo, as she watched her sister unfold it. "Well, what's Dick got to say?"

Madge glanced down the page of straggling writing

17

which had never lost its school-boyish characteristics. Then she gave vent to an exclamation.

"Oh, what *is* it?" demanded Jo, who was nearly dancing with impatience. "*Madge!* They aren't coming home are they?"

"He doesn't say so," replied Madge, who was pink with excitement. "It's—Joey, what do you think you are?"

"A genius," replied Joey promptly.

"Idiot! I didn't mean that," laughed her sister. "No! Listen!—and don't burst with excitement—you are an—*aunt!*"

"*What?*" Jo clutched her head.

"Listen!" And Madge read out, " 'Dear Kids,—The biggest joke in creation! You'll never believe it, and Mollie and I are still hooting over it. What do you think has happened? We've got twins! It's true! Boy and girl. Imagine us with twins! We can't believe it ourselves, and it's the joke of the season. One's dark like Moll, and the other's fair like me. Mollie is awfully happy, and I don't know whether I'm standing on my head or my heels. We are going to call them Margaret Josephine and Richard Geoffrey—to be known as Peggy and Rix."

"Well!!" gasped Jo, when her sister had got so far. "Isn't it just exactly like Dick and Mollie? Twins!"

"It's extraordinary!" agreed Madge. "They're calling the girl after us both. How nice of them!"

"She'll be another pupil for the Chalet School," said Jo, spinning round on her toes like a dancing dervish. "Hurrah! We are growing, aren't we?"

Madge broke into a peal of laughter. "Oh, Joey Bettany; you will be the death of me! Fancy talking of school for a baby not two months old. Why, it will be years and years before she is old enough for that."

"The Robin was only six," said Joey.

"There were special reasons for that," replied Madge quickly, and Joey said no more. The Robin, the school baby, had come to them a year ago, when her mother had died in decline, and her father, an English officer, had been obliged to leave her to go on business. She had settled down very happily among them, and had soon adopted her headmistress as an aunt; but neither of the Bettany girls could forget the tragedy which had touched her baby life, so Joey's remark had scarcely been a happy one.

Madge heard the sound of merry voices and a rush of

feet. "There are the girls!" she exclaimed. "Joey, run and tell Miss Carthew that I want them all to change at once— we don't want any more colds this term."

Joey grimaced expressively as she fled to the side door where the jolly crew were entering the house. The last part of her sister's speech had referred to herself and a bad cold she had caught on the previous Sunday. If it hadn't been for that cold, she would have gone with the others and have been arriving with them.

She gave the message to the mistress, who promptly sent the girls upstairs to change, and then turned into the study to report before she went across to her own quarters in the junior house, known as Le Petit Chalet, for the same purpose. As she left the room she met Jo, who was wandering back to her sister. The Bettanys were devoted to each other, and one of Jo's greatest grievances was that she could not see much of her sister during term time. "Miss Bettany was just going to send for you, Joey," she said with a smile. "She seems to want you rather specially."

"Thank you, Miss Carthew," said Joey. She waited for the mistress to pass, and then went in, to find her sister with a letter before her, a startled look on her delicate face.

"What on earth is the matter?" demanded Jo, wildly curious at once.

Miss Bettany turned to her. "Joey, I want you! Oh dear!" she went on, rather incoherently; "how everything does seem to happen at once!"

"What's happened now?" queried Jo.

The answer was sufficiently startling. "I am asked to take a princess as a pupil for next term."

"What!" Jo was too much surprised for politeness. "A *princess*? What princess?"

"Her father is the Crown Prince of Belsornia." Madge replied.

"Belsornia?" Jo frowned fiercely as she tried to remember where Belsornia was.

"Yes; it is one of the smaller Balkan States, not far from the Italian border," replied her sister. "This child—Princess Elisaveta—is the only child of the Crown Prince. She has been ill, it seems, and the doctor recommends school for her. This man—his secretary I suppose, and an Englishman evidently—has written asking for a prospectus, as the doctor advises sending her to us, Joey." She swung round

19

to her young sister. "What do you think? Can we manage with a princess in the school?"

"Rather! Why ever not?" demanded Joey, wide-eyed. "I should think it would be a jolly good thing for the school. Oh, take her, Madge. I'll see that she isn't sat on too much. But, I say! Why do you want *my* opinion? You aren't in the habit of asking my advice."

"I know." Miss Bettany looked serious. "The fact of the matter, Joey, is that though I shouldn't dream of asking you about the other girls as a general rule, yet in this case I must. I can't even consider the idea if it is going to upset the others, and some of them have a most exaggerated idea of royalty."

"Ask them to let her come as an ordinary girl, then," suggested Joey.

"I'll think over what you say," said Miss Bettany slowly. "In the meantime, say nothing about it. You will have heaps to tell the others, anyway, if you tell them about the twins. Remember, Joey. You must say *nothing* to anyone."

"Guide honour," replied Jo rapidly. "What did you say her name was?"

"Elisaveta. It is the Rumanian form of Elizabeth. I can't decide anything about it yet, Joey. She may never come. All the same——"

"All the same, it's an honour for the Chalet School," added Jo, as she turned to go and wash her hands and tidy her hair before *Mittagessen*.

Madge concurred with this opinion. "Yes; it *is* an honour for us. Run along, now, Joey Baba."

Joey trotted off, leaving her elder sister divided between pride and indecision. She wasn't sure just what to do. But it was an honour.

CHAPTER IV

MATRON!

"NINETEEN — twenty — twenty - one — twenty - two! All the face-towels are correct, Matron. What shall I do next?"

Matron, a little thin woman, with a face that Joey Bettany had declared to be exactly like a weasel's, finished

what she was doing, and then looked round at the speaker.
"Have you finished those, Jo? Then take yourself off. I
want no idle school-girls bothering round me when I am
busy. And take that child with you! She's nothing but a
pest and a torment!" She turned and picked up the towels,
marching off, leaving behind her a Joey literally speechless
with indignation.

At the end of last term, the matron Miss Bettany had
engaged a year before had left to go home and keep house
for a brother who had lost his wife, and was left with three
boys and a tiny girl. Miss Bettany had had too much to do
to go to England, and had engaged her new matron through
an agency. Miss Webb had arrived two days before, and
already the young Head was ruefully telling herself that she
had made a mistake *this* time. The new-comer was a little,
bustling woman, with a loud and unpleasant voice, a dom-
ineering manner, and an irritable temper. To the family
four—Madge, Joey, the Robin, and Juliet Carrick, the
headmistress's ward—Miss Webb was everything she ought
not to be.

Matron "could not do" with girls helping with the various duties. The three girls had always given a hand in the
somewhat strenuous period of getting ready for the new
term, and they were simply flabbergasted when one offer of
assistance after another was refused, or else accepted so
curtly as to take all the joy of helping out of everything
they did. However, Joey and Juliet were Guides, and the
Robin was a Brownie, so they did their level best to smile.
The Robin was rather pathetic about it, however. "Zoë, I
aren't a nuisance?" she said piteously, when she had had
some tablets of soap taken out of her hands with the remark, "Oh, go away and play outside, you little nuisance,
you!"

Jo's reply was not quite judicious. "Of course you're not,
darling! She's a cross old cat, and you're ever so much of
a help!"

Unfortunately for her, her sister heard her, and read her
a lecture on backing up authority to the juniors.

"I'm sorry if I've let you down, Madge," said the culprit;
"but she *is* cross, and it was horrid of her to call Robin a
nuisance when she isn't! She was only helping, just as we
always do."

"I cannot help that, Joey," said her sister gravely. "You
had no right to call her names to the baby. You know how

21

the Robin looks up to you and copies you in every way, and it was exceedingly naughty of you. If she tells the others, they will instantly take to all sorts of unpleasant names for Matron, and it will only make things more difficult."

"You *do* think she will give us an unpleasant term, then," said Jo shrewdly. "I am a beast, Madge! I didn't think of that. I won't call her names to the Robin any more. But it was awfully mean of her to say such things to our baby."

Madge Bettany sent Jo out to the little shop at the Post Hotel to get some picture post-cards that were wanted, and let the subject drop. All the same, she contrived to impress on Matron that the girls were accustomed to helping in the house out of term-time, and requested her not to interfere with them if she or Mademoiselle, or Miss Carthew, who had spent the holidays with them, should use the children in any way.

Matron heard her through to the end. Then she shrugged her shoulders. "Very well, Miss Bettany. Of course, you are mistress here, and it must be as you wish. All the same, I am not accustomed to having girls messing about when I am busy, and I don't like it. Also, I should prefer that they should not come into my province to carry tales about me."

Madge was furious. To begin with, there was a covert insolence in the Matron's manner to which she was quite unaccustomed. She was very young, she knew, to be a headmistress, and she looked much younger than she was. Nevertheless, she had never yet met with anything but the utmost respect from anyone. Apart from that, she was wildly indignant that such a charge as tale-bearing should be made against the three, more especially as not one of them had ever been guilty of such meanness.

However, she controlled herself, and said quietly, "I am sorry, Matron; but it is my wish that the girls should make themselves useful to those members of the staff whom I have mentioned, and I shall be glad if you will not interfere."

"Very well," replied Matron. "I will carry out your wishes."

The Robin soon recovered from Matron's tongue, and took care to keep out of that lady's way. It puzzled her, all the same. In all the seven years she had lived she had never met with anything but the tenderest love, and she had never dreamed that anyone could speak so unkindly when she was only trying to help. She referred the question to her beloved Jo. "It wasn't naughty, Zoë, was it?" she asked anxiously when the two were in bed that night. "I didn't never mean to be naughty. Tante Marguerite sent me with the soap. She truly did."

"It's all right, Bübchen; you weren't naughty a bit," declared Joey lovingly. "And, Robin, you mustn't repeat what I called Matron to the others, or it will make Madge unhappy. I shouldn't have said it to you."

"I won't tell the others," promised the Robin.

The door opened, and Matron came in. "Talking, Josephine?" she said. "What do you mean by keeping that child awake at this time of night? How dare you break the rules like this? I suppose that you think because the headmistress is your sister you can do as you like!"

Joey's temper flared up at this unfair accusation. "I wasn't breaking rules!" she said furiously. "School rules don't begin until Thursday. And I never behave like that— my sister wouldn't allow it, even if I thought of doing it!"

"Does she allow you to be impudent to older people?" snapped Matron.

"I wasn't impudent!" retorted Jo. "At any rate, I didn't mean to be. And it *is* true that school rules don't count in the holidays. My sister knows the Robin and I talk in bed then, and she doesn't mind, so long as we stop when Juliet comes up. We always sleep till eight in the morning, so it doesn't matter, she says."

Jo may not have meant any rudeness, but her tones certainly belied her in that case; and Miss Carthew, who was passing, may be forgiven if she thought that the child was "playing up" Matron. She came in quietly. "Joey," she said, "what do I hear you say?"

Jo was tongue-tied. Matron saw her chance, and rushed in. "This child is most impudent to me, Miss Carthew," she declared. "She is breaking the rules by talking after she has gone to bed; and when I come in to put a stop to it, she answers me in the rudest manner."

Miss Carthew did not like Matron any better than any of the others, but as a member of the staff, she was obliged to uphold her, so she replied, "Jo, I am surprised to hear this. You must apologise to Matron for your rudeness."

At this, no less a person than the Robin chimed in. "Zoë just told Matron that we didn't have school rules in holiday-time," she said.

23

"Matron did not know that," said Miss Carthew gravely. "Joey had no right to speak rudely to her.—Come, Jo! I am waiting. Apologise to Matron at once!"

If the Robin had not been there to notice all she said and did, Joey would have refused point-blank. As it was, with her sister's words ringing in her ears, she mumbled, "I'm sorry if I spoke rudely to you, Matron."

"I'm glad to hear it," replied Matron. "I will overlook it this time, but another time you will not get off so lightly, if I have anything to say in the matter." With that she rustled out, leaving an indignant trio behind her.

Miss Carthew knew better than to let the two children guess what she was feeling. She merely made them lie down, and tucked them up before she said, "Good-night, you two. Don't talk after Juliet comes up;" and left them.

Downstairs, however, she poured out her feelings to Mademoiselle. who sympathised with her. "The truth is, we have all got on so well up to this," declared Miss Carthew when she had spent her wrath, "that we don't quite know where we are when we meet with anything unpleasant. I backed her up, of course; but I'm convinced that Joey had some right on her side. Impertinence is not a failing of hers. If it had been that monkey, Grizel Cochrane, I shouldn't have been in the least surprised."

Upstairs, the pair most concerned lay in silence. Joey was trying to recover her temper, and the Robin was grieving because Jo had got into trouble. The baby adored the elder girl with her whole warm little heart. She looked up to Jo as an elder sister who petted her and looked after her, and any punishment of her idol meant sorrow to her. The people who had charge of the pair had soon found that the surest way of keeping Joey out of mischief was to remind her that the Robin was almost invariably heart-broken when she was in trouble. As Joey returned the baby's adoration, it was always a safe deterrent.

Juliet, coming up half an hour later in blissful ignorance of what had occurred, was so startled by the thick silence in the room that she nearly went for Madame, under the impression that the two must be ill. Then she saw the tears on the Robin's cheeks and the black scowl on Joey's brow, so she said nothing, but undressed and got to bed as fast as she could.

The next day Madge got the shock of her life when Joey begged to be set free from any more helping in the house.

When the Robin quite independently made the same request, and gave as her reason that she didn't want to be where Matron was, Miss Bettany realised that there were wheels within wheels here. She said nothing about it, however, merely keeping them employed for an hour or so in the school rooms, and then sending them out with Juliet for a ramble up the valley. It was very warm for the end of April, so she gave them sandwiches, cakes, and milk, and told them to stay out till tea-time. The weather had completely changed, and there was no fear of storms.

They had a glorious time together, making the most of this last day of the holidays. Tomorrow the boarders would arrive, and on the next day school would begin.

They came in to tea, which they had with Miss Bettany in the study, and then she chased them into a little room off the *Speisesaal*, where they found the walls were lined with open bookshelves, and there were piles of books standing about. "This is our library," explained the Head. "I have been wanting to arrange some sort of thing before this, but there has never been any chance. Now, Herr Mensch, Herr Marani, and Herr von Eschenau have sent me all these books as leaving gifts from Bernhilda, Gisela, and Wanda, so I got the men to put up these shelves, and brought all the books we had for the library in here. I want to get them all put in order tonight, and I thought you three would like to help me. Mademoiselle is busy with Matron, and Miss Carthew, Miss Maynard, and Miss Wilson are hard at work on the games time-table, so, if you can't help me, I must do it alone."

"We'll help, of *course!*" exclaimed the three. And help they did.

When everything was done, the Head sent the girls to get their *Abendessen*, telling her sister to come back to her in the study when she had finished. Matron passed them in the passage, but she took no notice of them, and Jo hurried through her meal, and was in the study in record time. "I'm here, Madge," she said.

Madge held out her hand. "Come and sit down beside me," she said.

Jo collapsed down beside her on the floor, laying her black head against her sister's knee. "Why do you want me, Madge?"

Madge made no reply at first, but simply sat there, her hand on the silky hair. "Joey," she said at length, "I want to ask you to be very careful this term. It is going to be a little bit difficult, I'm afraid. You see, we shall have Elisaveta, who has never been accustomed to anyone like Matron. Then we have Matron herself. I know she does not quite understand us yet, but I hope she soon will, and you can do a lot towards helping her to do so."

Joey wriggled uneasily. "Madge, I don't think so. Of course, I'll do as I'm told, and I won't say things before the little ones—if I can help it. But I—she doesn't like me, and she thinks I take advantage 'cos you're my sister."

"Did she say so?" asked Madge, startled.

"I—I didn't mean to say that," mumbled Joey. "Forget it, Madge; can't you?"

Madge nodded. "Yes. *We* know it isn't true, and that's all that really matters. Do your best, Joey. It's going to be the hardest term we've had yet, and I shall want all you can do to help. Remember, I've always trusted you as if you were grown-up, and I shall go on doing so. Avoid trouble with Matron, and help Elisaveta to be happy."

"Righto!!" replied Joey. Then she suddenly wriggled to her knees. "Madge, whisper! Isn't her voice *horrid?*"

"Hush, Joey! You mustn't say things like that."

"I sha'n't after to-night," replied Jo readily; "but *unofficially*, Madge, isn't it?"

Madge laughed. Then she gave in; it was safe enough with Jo. "Yes, Joey; it is trying. Whatever you do, don't develop one like it! And now we'll say no more about it. It is nearly nine o'clock, and there's a hard day before us to-morrow, you know. Kiss me, and run off to bed."

Joey got to her feet, and, flinging her arms round her sister's neck, bestowed on her a hug that completely disarranged her hair. "Good-night, Madge. You're a dear, and I love you!

Then she went off, and fell asleep, making all sorts of good resolutions for the coming term.

CHAPTER V

ELISAVETA IN TROUBLE

THE term was not three days old before Matron had succeeded in making herself the best-hated person in the Chalet School. The seniors all loathed her, and the middles ran whenever they saw her; the juniors, having next to nothing to do with her, were the best off, but even they fled round corners when they saw her in the distance. More and more Miss Bettany saw that she had made a bad mistake.

The staff said nothing to her, but a great deal amongst themselves.

Miss Maynard, as the senior member—Mademoiselle was a partner in the school—held the floor one evening when the lady under discussion was busy in the dormitories.

"It isn't only her voice," said the mathematics mistress; "it could be put up with if everything else weren't so bad. But her manner!"

"She seems to have taken a special dislike to Joey, the Robin, and that new child Elisaveta What's-her-name," put in Miss Durrant. "Why, I cannot see. They're three of the most harmless children we possess."

"I can explain Joey, anyhow," said Miss Carthew. "She thinks Madame favours her because Jo is her sister."

"What rot!" cried Miss Wilson. "Why, Madame is stricter with Jo than with anyone else. And that doesn't explain her dislike of the Robin. I never thought *anyone* could do anything but like her. She's a dear little thing!"

"Of course, it's easy to see why she detests Elisaveta," observed Miss Durrant. "It's that little princess air of hers that riles the good lady so much."

"Yes.—What do *you* make of Elisaveta Arnsonira?" inquired Miss Maynard.

"How do you mean?" asked Miss Durrant.

"Well—she's not our type of child, is she?"

"No; now you mention it, she isn't. But except for that

funny air of being one of the royal family of somewhere, there isn't anything you can take hold of."

She got up as she spoke, and went towards the door. Just as she opened it, there was the most surprising sound to be heard, coming along the passage. It was the sound of someone dragging someone else forcibly along.

The mistresses all turned to the door with deep curiosity, and through it came Matron, half-dragging, half-carrying Elisaveta, Princess of Belsornia.

"Matron!" cried Miss Maynard. "What does this mean?"

"Mean?" repeated Matron, releasing her victim, who stood with furious anger in her face. "Mean? It means, Miss Maynard, that as Miss Bettany is out, I have brought this insolent child to you to punish as she deserves!"

"Very well, Matron," replied Miss Maynard quietly. "You may leave her, and I will attend to the matter at once."

"Not before I've told my story," retorted Matron.

"Certainly, I will hear your side of the matter. What has Elisaveta been doing?"

"She flew at me because I reproved Josephine Bettany for her untidiness and also for her impertinence to me, and she actually told me that I was no lady to speak as I did!" declared Matron, who, truth to tell, rather bore out the validity of Elisaveta's accusation by her present manner.

"I see. Is this true, Elisaveta?"

"Quite true, Madame," replied Elisaveta, standing with her head proudly, and her eyes flashing.

"Then you must apologise to Matron for your rudeness," said Miss Maynard.

"I regret!" Elisaveta was all princess now. "That, I cannot do."

"You see!" Matron waved to Miss Maynard. "She is thoroughly impertinent and insubordinate."

"Go to your room, Elisaveta." Miss Maynard waited, and Elisaveta meekly turned and went off to her room. "I will see her in private, Matron. In the meantime, I must go and attend to something. She will be better for being left alone for the present."

"Yes; if she is locked in!"

The mistress shook her head. "We never lock the girls in at this school."

"There will be no thought of locking in Elisaveta or any other girl," said Miss Maynard. "Madame would not allow

28

it. And while I remember, Matron, would you please call the headmistress "Madame," as we all do. It is her own wish."

Matron flounced out of the room, muttering something about "such rubbish!"

"What a woman!" exclaimed Miss Wilson. "What are you going to do with the child, Maynie?"

"Try to make her see reason," replied Miss Maynard. "I want her version of the story."

"Better get Joey's as well," suggested Miss Carthew. "There must have been a scene of sorts. She always looks as though she was scared of her own shadow."

"I might," agreed Miss Maynard. "Yes; I think I'll do that first."

She went out of the room, and up to the Yellow dormitory, where she was pretty sure of finding Joey, since Matron had been finding fault with her for untidiness. As she reached the door, she heard the harsh voice saying, "Put that drawer right at once, and you can take an order-mark for leaving it in such a disgraceful condition. *I* don't make any differences for the Head's sister, as you may just as well realise! Every time I find your drawers in a mess like this I shall punish you, so remember!"

The mistress entered the room, to find Joey with a mutinous expression on her face turning out the contents of a drawer which looked as if it had been well stirred up with a stick. There had certainly been some grounds for Matron's complaint!

"May I speak to Joey, Matron?" asked Miss Maynard.

"Yes, Miss Maynard. And I wish you would speak to her about her untidiness while you are about it!" replied Matron vigorously. "Just look at that drawer!"

"It is disgraceful," said Miss Maynard sternly. "When I have finished with you, Joey, you must come back and put everything in its proper place. I will come and inspect it myself before you go to bed. Now come with me."

Joey followed her out of the room and into the little bedroom across the landing which was hers. Miss Maynard gave her a chair, and perched herself on the bed. "Joey, what was the cause of Elisaveta's being so rude to Matron?"

Joey twisted her fingers together, and stared at the ground.

"Come, Joey! I want to know. Elisaveta must apologise

29

to Matron, of course, but I want to know why she was so rude."

"It was my fault, I suppose," said Jo at length. "My drawer *was* untidy, and Matron was angry, and she said— things. Then Elisaveta got angry too, and she said Matron hadn't the—the instincts of a lady, or she wouldn't have said such things—it was only *canaille* who spoke so. Matron was *wild*, and she carted her off to Mad—I mean, my sister, and—and that's about all."

"What did Matron say that made Elisaveta interfere?" asked Miss Maynard, her eyes on Jo's face.

Jo suddenly flushed. "I'm not going to repeat such a thing," she said. "It's an insult to Madge to even think it!"

"Was it the same sort of thing as I heard her saying when I came to find you?" asked the mistress.

Joey sat dumb.

"Tell me, Joey," insisted Miss Maynard. "I mean to know—or leave it to Madame!"

That told at once. Joey had no idea of letting her sister be dragged into the affair. She lifted her head, and Miss Maynard almost gasped at the fury in her eyes as she said, "She said that my sister favoured me because I *was* her sister, and the Robin and Juliet because they were her wards, and *she* wasn't going to, and we should all see that, and——"

"That will do," said Miss Maynard very quietly, though inwardly she was rather horrified by the storm that had been raised. "You must try to control yourself, Joey. You will only upset yourself and Madame if you give way to anger like this."

"I—I'd like to *kill* her!" burst out Joey.

"Nonsense, child! You wouldn't do anything of the sort, and it is very silly of you to say so." Miss Maynard paused. Under the circumstances, she did not think it would be very wise to let Joey go back to her tidying. She made up her mind quickly. "I want you to go over to Le Petit Chalet for me," she said. "I will give you a note to Mademoiselle, and you must wait for an answer."

Going to her table, she opened her letter-pad, and hastily scribbled, "Keep Joey with you for the present. She is upset." Folding this up, she gave it to Jo, and saw her trotting off to the other house, already a little calmer. Then she turned away, and went downstairs to the Blue dormitory on the next landing.

30

There was no defiance to meet here. Elisaveta was lying on her bed, crying heart-brokenly. She never heard the mistress enter the room, and only looked up when a hand was laid on her shoulder, and a quiet voice said, "Elisaveta, get up." She tumbled to the floor, and stood there, a piteous little object, for she had scrubbed her eyes in a way that would have made Alette shriek with horror. "You have been a very silly child," said Miss Maynard gently. "Whatever Matron said to Joey, you had no business to interfere. I know you only did it through friendship, but that is the sort of thing that friends must not do. Now, you have been rude to Matron, who is many years older than yourself, and in authority over you as well. I am sorry, Elisaveta, but you must come with me and apologise to her." Then, seeing that Elisaveta was about to refuse, she added, "You *must*. You were in the wrong in that way, and it is what a lady would do."

Elisaveta gave a final scrub to her eyes with a very damp pocket-handkerchief, and then said with a hiccup, "I—I'll come."

"Wash your face first," said Miss Maynard kindly.

Elisaveta did as she was told, and splashed vigorously with cold water till the tear-stains were fairly well washed away. Then she went with Miss Maynard to Matron's room, where she said, as if she were repeating a lesson, "I am sorry I was rude to you, Matron, and I beg your pardon."

She had barely got the words out before Miss Maynard bundled her through the door, and Matron was left with words of admonition on her lips.

"I couldn't help it," she said afterwards to her colleagues in the staff-room. "I remembered what happened when Joey had to apologise to her, and I felt I couldn't stand it."

To Miss Bettany, to whom she gave a strictly unofficial account of the affair, she said, "*Do* relieve our curiosity! Who is that child?"

Miss Bettany looked a little shamefaced. "I suppose it was idiotic of me not to tell you all in the beginning. She is the only child of the Crown Prince of Belsornia!"

"Good heavens! And Matron has been pitching into her as if she were just anyone. No wonder she told her she wasn't lady-like!"

They both laughed. "Tell the others," said Miss Bettany as the mistress got up to go. "But don't let the girls know."

CHAPTER VI

THE S.S.M. IS FORMED

MISS Bettany had Matron into the study, and informed her that no girl was ever forcibly dragged to any mistress; nor was any girl to be accused by any member of the staff of taking advantage of the Head. Matron listened to her with a sniff. "Very well, Miss Bettany," she said when Madge had finished.

"Another thing, Matron," replied the Head. "I notice you do not call me 'Madame', as the rest of the staff do. I shall be glad if you will follow their example."

Matron bowed her head, but she said nothing, and got herself out of the room as quickly as she could.

"Oh dear!" sighed Madge when she had gone. "*What* a term we are in for!"

The girls were quick to seize on Miss Webb's peculiarities. She was unlike anyone they had ever had to do with in the school and they proceeded to give her a bad time of it. The ringleader was Margia Stevens, who combined musical ability and original sin in a remarkable manner. Her followers were Evadne Lannis, an American child, Paula von Rothefels, Ilonka Barcokz, Sophie Hamel, and Suzanne Mercier. This sextette managed amongst them to give Matron a time of it.

Margia, possessed of a good deal of originality, thought out the most unheard-of things, and the others helped her to carry them out.

A week after Elisaveta's scrape with Matron, Margia approached her during the twenty minutes' break in the middle of the morning. "I say," she said, "would you come to the pine-woods after *Mittagessen?*"

"Why?" demanded Elisaveta, whose mind had leapt back to her beloved stories, and who therefore suspected something. "What do you want with me?"

"You'll see when you get there," replied Margia mysteriously. "I may say," she added, "that it's something to do with our unnatural tyrant."

"Matron?"

"Thou hast said rightly, oh damsel."

"All right, I'll come," agreed the "damsel"; and Margia went off, satisfied that she had secured another member for her band.

When finally *Mittagessen* was over, and they were dismissed for the hour's free time which they always had in the summer at this hour, most of the middles decamped with the utmost speed. Margia and her satellites made for the pine-woods, where they were allowed to go during the afternoon and the early evening. Elisaveta waited till most people had disappeared, and then she went slowly down the playing-field to the pine-woods which covered the mountains behind the house, keeping in the shade of the hedge of thorn-bushes which Herr Braun had had set there in order to keep off inquisitive people. She found the little wicket-gate at the bottom of the field open, and in the distance she could hear the voices of the others coming from among the trees. She followed the sound, and presently came upon Evadne Lannis, who was standing at attention, a long willow-wand in her hand.

"Halt! " said the sentinel. "Whither wouldst thou go?"

"Margia told me to come here," replied the maiden, with an involuntary giggle.

Evadne usually spoke the most picturesque American slang, and, despite nearly two years at the Chalet School, where slang was taboo, she was always coming out with some unheard-of expression, so this prim mode of address was very funny from her.

Evadne frowned at the giggle, but she held out her wand, and said, "Hold, and I will lead thee to the Presence!"

Elisaveta took hold of the wand, and was towed through the trees towards a little corner specially affected by the middles.

Elisaveta presently found herself ushered into "the Presence." Margia was seated on a heap of twigs over which was thrown the remnants of an old cubicle curtain. It was only possible to know that she *was* Margia by her pink cotton frock and the thick curly mop of hair. Her face was hidden by a hideous paper mask, and this was crowned by a wreath of alpen roses. Elisaveta stopped short and stared at this hideous vision, as well she might. Margia suppressed an evident tendency to giggle, and said in a deep voice, "Hail, maiden! Who art thou?"

Elisaveta recognised an event from her beloved school-stories, and thrilled with joy as she replied, "I am Elisaveta of Belsornia."

There was a gasp. *"Who* did you say?" demanded Margia in her natural tones.

"Er—I mean, Elisaveta Árnsonira," stammered Elisaveta, realising that, in her excitement, she had let the cat out of the bag.

"That wasn't what you said at first," declared Margia. "Explain your meaning, my love, or you don't join us, I can tell you! The S.S.M. doesn't have any secrets—I mean its members don't. If you want to be one of us, and I think you ought, you've jolly well got to tell us why you gave your name in such a funny way at first."

Elisaveta thought rapidly. "I'll tell you, if you'll swear not to tell the others," she said finally.

"Righto! Consider it done!" returned Margia amiably.

"Well then, my father is the Crown Prince of Belsornia."

There was a little silence, broken by Evadne, who gave vent to a long whistle. "I say, you aren't—er—sticking us?" she queried.

"I tell the truth," returned Elisaveta, lifting her head proudly.

"Oh, all right! I didn't mean to get your goat. Only it seems such a *rum* thing to happen in a school! I thought all princesses had governesses and things!"

"I had," replied the Princess ruefully. "There were three of them, and I hated them, really. But after I was ill the doctor said I was to come to school, so I came."

"Well, it's a jolly good thing for you that you came here," declared Margia. "This is the decentest school in the world, and you ought to have a rip—er—*splendid* time here, if you're decent yourself."

"Aren't we going to get on with the meeting?" suggested Ilonka, a Hungarian child. "The bell will be going for afternoon work if we do not make haste."

There was wisdom in her words, and the little assembly pulled itself together, and Margia, having resumed her former dignity, inquired, "Why comest thou?"

"Because you told me to do so," replied Elisaveta promptly.

" 'Tis well. Wilt thou be one of us? We are sworn to be the bitter enemies of Matron, and to harry her till she leaves the place. We are the Society for the Suppression of Matron. Wilt thou become one of us?"

Elisaveta flushed. "Yes, I will," she said firmly.

"Then take the oath. The Lady of the Revels will administer it."

The Lady of the Revels—Suzanne Mercier—stepped forward. "Hold up both thy hands and repeat this after me," she said impressively.

Elisaveta held up both arms to the pine branches above her, and duly repeated after her: "I, Elisaveta Margherita of Belsornia, do swear by the trees, the mountains, and the Tiern See that I will do everything in my power to make our present Matron's life a burden to her, and to make her leave us."

This interesting ceremony had just been completed when Joey Bettany appeared on the scene, looking furious.

"That *beast* Matron has been ragging the Robin!" choked Joey. "She made her cry, and then when the Robin told her that she had nothing to do with *her* drawers, Matron marched her off to the study to my sister, and she had to scold the baby for being rude to Matron, and send her to bed as a punishment. Robin said she would say she was sorry, to please Madame, but she didn't mean it; so now the poor babe's been shoved off to bed, and it's all Matron's fault. The Robin never cheeked anyone in her life before, and I'm jolly sure she wouldn't have done it now if Matron hadn't been such a *pig!*"

What else Joey might have had to say on the subject they did not hear, for at that moment the headmistress appeared among them. "Jo, were you using slang?" she asked briefly.

"Yes," replied Jo.

"Forbidden slang?"

"Yes."

"I am sorry. You know the rule as well as I do, I think. Well, I shall have to punish you, and you know that I dislike punishing anyone. Go to your dormitory, take your Milton with you, and learn by heart his sonnet to 'Cyriack Skinner.'"

"Please, Madame, I was talking slang too," said Margia.

"Then I am ashamed of you both. You are two girls who have been longest in the school, and I should have thought you would have remembered my wishes on the subject. You may take the same punishment as Josephine. Repeat the poem to me after *Kaffee*. Now you may go."

"It was me, too," said Evadne.

"The same thing applies to you. Have any of you other girls been breaking the rule as well?"

They hastily searched their memories, but Margia spoke up for them. "No, Madame."

"Just as well," said Miss Bettany in chilling tones. "Go now, you three."

They went dejectedly, and the headmistress followed them. She was half-way across the field when she heard the sound of hurrying steps behind her. She turned round. Elisaveta was running after her with a flushed face. "If you please, Madame, may I speak to you?" she panted.

"Yes, of course," replied the young Head, wondering if Elisaveta were going to confess to having spoken slang also, though Margia had seemed positive that no one but the three had done so.

"It is that I have told the girls that I am a princess," said Elisaveta. "I didn't mean to, but it slipped out."

Miss Bettany looked at her thoughtfully. "What did they say?" she asked.

"That it was lucky for me that I had been allowed to come to the Chalet School," replied the Princess promptly. "They promised they wouldn't tell the others," she added.

"Don't broadcast it, Elisaveta. As it turns out, it doesn't matter so much. It was mainly on your own account that your father and I thought it better the girls should not know. I was afraid it might make them a little stiff with you. If they only think, however, that you have been lucky to escape from governesses to school, it won't make any difference."

"No," agreed Elisaveta.

"Are you having a good time?" queried the Head.

"Splendid!" was the reply. Elisaveta *did* think she was having a good time when she was invited to become a member of a secret society. It was *just* like the stories. Miss Bettany nodded as she looked at her new pupil. There could be no doubt that she was settling down quite happily, despite Matron, and she already looked a very different child from the one who had been brought to Briesau by Mademoiselle de Séguiné ten days ago. There was nothing suppressed or tired about this long-legged school-girl, with her thick curls tied back with an untidy bow, and her short blue cotton frock all crumpled and stained with ink.

"You are not very tidy," she said. "I think you had better go and change your frock before we begin the afternoon work. Give that one to Marie, and she will try to take the inkstains out for you. And don't use your frocks as penwipers!"

Meanwhile Elisaveta mounted the stairs to the yellow dormitory to change her frock, a deep admiration for this mistress, who did not seem to worry unduly over crumples and inkstains, welling up within her. She felt that she would do anything to please Miss Bettany.

In the dormitory she found Margia struggling with John Milton's tribute to Cyriack Skinner, rebellion in her heart. Not against the Head—oh dear, no! The person Margia blamed for her incarceration was Matron.

She went to have her task heard after *Kaffee* in no penitent mood, and Miss Bettany guessed as much. "I'm afraid you aren't really sorry, Margia," she said.

"I'm sorry if you are angry with me," said Margia frankly, "but not for anything else."

"I'm not angry," replied the headmistress. "I *am* rather disappointed to find you are so lacking in self-control, but that's all. Run away, now, and send Jo to me."

Margia dropped her regulation curtsy and fled. The Head's remarks hurt her a good deal more than a scolding would have done, and it was one more charge to be laid up against Matron.

Jo, who was the last one, went to her sister, inwardly dreading her reception. She knew perfectly well that any breach of the rules was more serious in her than in any other girl, and, contrary to Miss Webb's opinion, it was the rarest thing in the world for her to take any advantage of her relationship to the Head. She found her sister standing looking out of the window. "I know the sonnet, Madame," she said nervously. She dared not use the Christian name till she knew how her sister was feeling.

Miss Bettany put the proffered book gently aside. "I won't bother to hear it," she said. "I shall say nothing further about what occurred this afternoon—I don't think it's necessary."

"It isn't," agreed Jo.

"All I want to ask you is to try to put up with Matron. The Robin was really very very naughty to say what she did! She deserved her punishment."

"Do you know, Joey," said her sister solemnly, "I begin to think that it's a very good thing that we have Miss Webb with us for a short time, at least."

37

Jo sat back on her heels and regarded her sister and if she thought she had gone mad.

"Yes; I mean it!" Madge nodded her pretty head. "Everything has gone so smoothly with us since we started, that it's just as well we should realise that there must be difficulties sometimes."

"I don't think it's always been so easy as all that," replied Jo. "There was the time when Grizel and I were lost on the Tiern-joch; and when I dished my ankle at the ice carnival last year; and the flood; and measles last term. It hasn't always been 'everything-in-the-garden's-lovely' by any means."

"No; I agree with you. But where we *have* been singularly fortunate is in our staff."

"Yes. That's so."

"Now, Joey, you must try to remember that Matron is in authority—a certain amount—over you all. I have given her that authority, and you can surely trust me to see that it isn't abused. So I want you to control your temper. Understand?"

Jo nodded. "Um. But it's horribly difficult sometimes."

As soon as she had gone, the Head put down the letters she had been playing with and went over to Le Petit Chalet, where the Robin was crying herself to sleep, broken-hearted because "Tante Marguerite" was angry with her.

A little talk, and a lot of cuddling soon put her all right again, and she dropped off, happy at last. Miss Bettany left her when she was safely in the land of dreams, and went to Mademoiselle's study. "Mademoiselle," she said as she collapsed into a chair, "I'm becoming a preaching bad-tempered head-mistress, and I don't know what to do."

Mademoiselle, who had known the Bettany girls for years, and loved them both dearly, looked at her young Head. "It is that woman, Miss Webb," she said shrewdly. "Well, *ma chérie,* do not vex yourself. It can but last for the term, and already we have passed ten days. Let us consider, instead, if it will be well to make Margia Stevens do all her own mending. She has torn yet another dress."

CHAPTER VII

THE MIDDLES ARE REVENGED

FOR a full week after that, the membership of the S.S.M. rather languished.

There were so few rules in the school that, as a rule, punishments were not often needed. The one about the use of slang had been absolutely necessary, since it was not to be expected that the mothers of girls who were not English would be pleased if their daughters picked up vocabularies of English slang. The others were based on the same principle. It was an English school, so English had to be spoken during school-hours, except during lessons in other languages; the girls were not supposed to speak at all after "lights out"; the little ones were forbidden to play by the lakeside or on the banks of the little stream which flowed through the valley, without special permission. These were the bulk of the regulations, and the slang one was the one most frequently broken.

Matron tried to enforce a few of her own. They mainly related to tidiness, mending, and so on; but one she did make, and which proved very unpopular, had to do with the Sunday morning reading. On Sundays the rising-bell did not ring until half-past eight. Several of the girls awoke at their usual hour—seven o'clock—and the Head had always given permission for them to have story-books by their beds on this one morning in the week, so that they might read if they wanted to pass the time that way. Matron now put a stop to this. On the second Saturday night she confiscated all books she found in the dormitories; and when the girls protested that they had always done it, she snapped out, "Then it ceases from this term! If you wake up, you may lie awake and rest yourselves. There is going to be no more reading in bed; so don't let me catch any of you with books in your cubicles after this!"

Funnily enough, the school took it for granted that Miss Bettany had decided this, and they knew better than to make a complaint if that was the case. No one, afterwards, could explain how this had been decided. The fact remained that the girls grumbled among themselves, but otherwise took it quietly.

Jo was the one most affected. She had a trick of waking very early, and as it was, always lay awake for an hour or more, since the headmistress had forbidden reading before seven o'clock. Lying awake, tossing restlessly from side to side for a couple of hours or more was no rest, and she always got up on Sundays tired out to begin with.

This went on for three Sundays without the Head noticing it. Then, one Sunday, it struck her that her little sister was looking very shadowy about the eyes, and she made inquiries as to the reason for it. "Why are you looking so tired, Joey?" she asked during the afternoon, when she always had Joey with her for an hour or two. "Your eyes are like saucers and you are as white as a sheet. Haven't you been sleeping?"

"Yes; but I do so hate lying awake till the rising-bell with nothing to do," explained Joey.

"Nothing to do!" exclaimed Madge. "Then what has become of all your books? Don't tell me that you have read everything in the library yet, because I shan't believe it!"

"Of course I haven't," said Jo indignantly. "But that's a lot of use to me when you've put an end to reading on Sunday mornings!"

"When I've—*what?*" gasped Madge, sitting bolt upright.

"Didn't you?" demanded Joey.

"Put an end to the Sunday morning reading? No; I certainly have *not*. I'm afraid I must have said something to lead Matron to think that I wished it to be stopped," said Madge, who knew very well she had done nothing of the sort, as the question had never arisen. "I will tell Matron that I never meant anything of the kind."

She changed the subject after that, and they said no more about it; but Joey took care to explain to the others that the order had been originated by Matron, and that the headmistress had had nothing to do with it.

The indignation in the school was great.

The S.S.M. called a meeting as soon as possible, and decided that this last offence must not go unpunished. Had they but known it, Miss Bettany had given Matron a bad half-hour in the study already, for she was seriously annoyed at the whole affair.

Margia summoned a meeting under the pines, and invited certain people from the middles to join them. Joey, Elisaveta, Frieda Mensch, Simone Lecoutier, and Bianca di Ferrara all accepted, and a rowdy gathering met and vowed that Matron should be taught the proper way of treating the Head of the school.

"All those who agree that we should try to get Matron to shove off, hands up!" cried Evadne excitedly.

Every hand went up.

"*Good!*" said Margia. "Now, be quiet for a few minutes, and everyone think of something to do to her."

They settled down to think, and there was a little silence. Elisaveta was the first to speak. "I have thought," she said plaintively. "How much longer do you others want?"

"I've got an idea, too," said Ilonka. "Hurry up, you people!"

"We've all had time to think," decreed Margia. "Now, don't all yell at once. Paula, you're the oldest; carry on, and tell us what your idea is."

"I think we ought to make a—how do you say it?—a booby-trap on her door," said Paula, who was not famed for originality, and had got this idea from her library-book.

"And have her asking who did it, and dragging Madame into it again!" said the president of the society contemptuously. "Talk sense!"

Paula retired, crushed; and Sophie Hamel made her suggestion: "Let's nail her window down."

Margia sighed. "I wish you'd all use your brains a little. I hope no one's going to be idiotic enough to suggest an apple-pie bed. We must have something *subtle*. She'd know at once that some of us had done it—she isn't *touched!*"

After that scathing remark nobody was anxious to make any suggestions. It was difficult, when you came to think of it, to fix on something which Matron wouldn't at once lay to their account. Finally, Elisaveta made a suggestion which was the best so far. "Let's tie something on a string and dangle it out of the Blue dormitory window so that it keeps tapping against her window," she proposed. "If we could do it during the night it would have a weird sound."

"Not bad," agreed the president.

What else she would have said remained buried in oblivion, for at that moment Joey Bettany leaped to her feet with a shout of, "Eureka! I've got it!"

"Oh, what?" cried the united S.S.M.

For reply Joey turned to Simone Lecoutier. "Simone,

41

d'you remember what I told you about the time when Madame and the Robin and I went to stay with Maynie in the New Forest?"

Simone nodded, her face flushing with excitement. *"Mais oui*—I mean, yes! You said it was 'orrrrreeble!'" she cried eagerly, putting an extra number of r's into the last word, and becoming extra French over the memory.

"What was it!" demanded Margia "You've never told *us.*"

"It was *gruesome!*" declared Jo with a little shiver at the memory. "It was at three o'clock in the morning, and I woke 、) to hear the most ghastly squealing sounds just outside the window. It had wakened the Robin, too, and we were frozen with horror! I was too scared to speak. It sounded like—like a soul in torment. Luckily, the Robin let out the most awful squall, and my sister heard—she was sleeping next door. She came dashing in, under the impression that one of us was being killed, and then we discovered what it was. A snail had got on to the glass somehow, and was creeping down. You know how they hump their bodies in the middle, and then spread out to move on? Well, that was what it was doing, and anything more uncanny I never want to hear!"

"And you think it would be a jolly good thing to do with Matron? I do, too," said Margia eagerly. "Let's go and catch snails after *Kaffee*. There are dozens in the garden. We can take one upstairs and stick it on the window, and she'll never know that it didn't get there on its own."

"But how will you put it on the window?" asked Frieda, who possessed most of the common-sense of the society. "It is too far up to reach it from the ground, and too far below the window of the Blue dormitory for Jo or Elisaveta or Bianca to stretch down."

"Oh, we'll manage somehow," declared Jo, who was delighted with her own scheme. "Trust me for that!"

After *Kaffee* that afternoon the middles trotted off to the garden and had a snail hunt. They got six fat ones, which, for the present, were relegated to a box in Margia's drawer, and then they went off to cricket practice with the air of archangels.

At eleven o'clock that night the window of the Blue dormitory was cautiously pushed up to its farthest extent, and three faces looked out. For once fortune had favoured them. Eigen, the boy-of-all-work, had been touching up the fresco which adorned the walls here, and he had left his ladder standing against the side of the house. It was an easy matter for three active-school-girls to climb over the balcony and get on to the nearest rung. From that it was a mere step to get to Matron's window, where Jo reconnoitred cautiously before she proceeded any farther. Matron was lying asleep, snoring lustily. Jo held out her hand, and took the snail Elisaveta handed to her with a little shudder. Then she put it on the window-pane, holding it for a minute until it had had a chance to stick to the glass.

"Now me," insisted Elisaveta. "I want to do one."

Joey amiably climbed farther down the ladder, and the Princess affixed her slimy pet to the glass. Then the three went softly back up the ladder, and managed to climb back to the balcony without breaking their legs or arms in the process.

"Even if she thinks it's us, she won't be able to swear to it," said Jo, with a low chuckle—"What are you doing, Elisaveta?"

"Going to make sure she won't," replied Elisaveta as she pushed the ladder outwards.

It fell with a soft thud into the long grass, but, luckily for them, it woke no one, though it did disturb Matron, who rolled over on to her side, half-opening her eyes as she did so. She was not fully roused, however, and the trio got back into bed before anything further happened. They were all nearly asleep, when the Chalet was suddenly awakened by a wild yell. Another and another followed. There was a sound of opening doors and scurrying feet, and then Miss Bettany's voice was heard, demanding to know what was the matter.

The wicked three tumbled out of bed once more and joined the agitated crowd on the stairs. They were rewarded by seeing Matron, clad only in her nightdress, and with her hair in curling-pins, rush out on to the lower landing, crying that her room was haunted by murderers!

Margia who had emerged from the Yellow dormitory just in time to hear this, caught Elisaveta's eye, and went off into a fit of smothered laughter.

In the meantime, Miss Bettany had boldly ventured into the room, and at once realised what had happened. "It's all right, Matron," she said. "It's only two snails who have been promenading down the window-pane. There they are."

She pointed them out, and the room was instantly

crowded by people who wanted to see the disturbers of the peace.

Jo and Elisaveta were among them, and Joey had the presence of mind to exclaim, "Oh, isn't that just exactly what happened to the Robin and me in England! Do you remember, Madame? It was horrid!"

"Two of them!" said Miss Maynard, innocently helping her out. "That is one worse than you, Joey."

"One was bad enough," declared Jo. *"Two* must be awful! Shall I knock them off it into the grass?"

"It would be as well," agreed her sister. "I wonder how they got up there?"

"Who can fathom the ways of snails?" laughed Miss Maynard.

Nobody tried to answer her, and Miss Bettany sent the girls all back to bed the next minute, so they heard no more. Matron went back to her room, feeling annoyed with herself for having made such a fuss about such a little thing, and peace once more settled down on the Chalet School.

CHAPTER VIII

THE FEUD CONTINUES

NO one was blamed for the snails' curious choice of a promenade. Joey's speech about the occurrence while they had been at the Maynards's had completely thrown her sister off the scent, and though Matron had her suspicions, she could scarcely suggest that the girls were to blame for it. Moreover, Miss Bettany had snubbed her so severely over the stopping of the Sunday morning reading, that she felt that she had better lie low for a while. As for the S.S.M., they were so delighted with themselves that the wonder was that they did not give themselves away wholesale.

"It was a *topping* rag!" announced Margia enthusiastically at their next meeting. "If we can only push a few more like that on to her, we shall soon get rid of her. What can we do next?"

"Better wait a while," said Jo practically. "If things happen too often, she'll get suspicious—not that that would be anything fresh for her!" she added.

"I've thought of a *lovely* plan!" cried Elisaveta. "It won't be *at* her, exactly. But Madame will set it down to her."

"I doubt it!" remarked Jo feelingly. "She's all there—my sister. It'll have to be a jolly good thing to get her to blame *her* and not *us* for anything we do."

"She will this, though," retorted the Princess, who was sitting in a most un-princess-like attitude, with her feet on her desk. They were in their form-room at the time. "It's just this. Let's all begin to talk like Matron!"

A grin of pure delight illumined Joey's features at the idea. She knew her sister's ideas on the subject of voices. Miss Bettany herself had a low, musical voice, and if there *was* anything she disliked more than another in Matron, it was the loud, harsh tones in which she invariably spoke. If the entire middle school began to copy them, Jo foresaw trouble of all kinds coming to them. All the same, it was a really beautiful chance, so she contented herself by saying, "Well, I hope you're prepared to write out that thing of Shakespeare's about

"Her voice was ever sweet, gentle, and low,
    An excellent thing in woman"

umpteen times; for that's what will happen to us!"

"We must begin gradually," said Elisaveta, warming up as she went on to explain the details of her plan. "If we all start shouting at once, they will know it is on purpose."

Joey nodded thoughtfully. "That's true.—You really are a brain, Elisaveta. We'd better begin—just two or three of us—by degrees. The others can join in later."

"I reckon it's *our* turn to shine," said Evadne. "You three did the snails stunt, so some of the rest of us ought to get busy with this first."

"Well, you and Suzanne and Ilonka and me," said Margia. "Then you others by degrees. I shall have to remember to shout."

45

They were careful not to begin that day—it was too soon after what Evadne called "the snails stunt." Next morning Suzanne was called to order twice for speaking loudly, and Ilonka was warned that if she couldn't moderate her tones, she would be put into silence at meal-times.

In the afternoon Mr Denny, the school singing-master, came to give them their bi-weekly lesson. He was a dreamy, irresponsible being, who declared that all teaching should be based on Plato's—that is, that music should have the first place in every school. The girls had christened him "Plato," because he talked so much about the great philosopher, and liked him very much.

This afternoon it seemed good to them to give him a taste of what was coming. They did not dare do much, for Mademoiselle was accompanying them, but at the end of the afternoon, when the master was saying "Good-bye" to Miss Maynard, whom he chanced to meet in the passage, he said, in rather bewildered tones, "What has chanced to make our little maids so noisy to-day?"

"How do you mean?" asked Miss Maynard quickly.

"They seem to have forgotten their soft voices, and adopted a louder tone which is hurtful to the ear," he explained.

"*All* of them?" queried the mistress.

"Plato" thought a minute. "Nay; not all. But some spoke in strident tones which I do not like. Perchance they are excited over some girlish trifle."

"Perhaps they are," agreed Miss Maynard non-committally.

He went off after that; and Miss Maynard, left to herself, put in some hard thinking. Miss Bettany had gone away for the weekend to interview her lawyers at Innsbruck about some business. She had gone that afternoon, and would spend the Saturday with Frieda Mensch's people, going to Maria Marani's for the Sunday, and returning early on Monday morning. Joey had known of this, and it had seemed to her to be a good opportunity for beginning the latest campaign.

At *Kaffee*, which the girls always had by themselves, Miss Maynard wandered into the *Speisesaal* under some slight pretext; but there was nothing to worry her then. They were all talking in their usual manner. She decided that the singing-master must have had a bad attack of imagination, and went her way, relieved and grateful. The next day was Saturday, and Guide parade. The Chalet School company was not a large one, but they were all very keen. Work, this term, consisted in badge-work, the making and furnishing of a big doll's house—which was destined for one of the children's hospitals in Vienna—and special drills. As Miss Bettany, the Guide captain, was away, the girls spent most of their time on the doll's house. Miss Maynard, as the lieutenant, supervised all the work, and went from one to another giving advice, and helping where it was necessary. She was dismayed to notice that in one or two of the girls there was a tendency to speak roughly, and Evadne was screeching away with Suzanne, Ilonka, and Margia as good seconds. They stopped as soon as she spoke to them; but they soon forgot, and went on again. Even Margia appeared to be losing her soft voice, and talked at the full pitch of her lungs.

The S.S.M. exchanged glances of congratulation as they noted the mistress's face. The plan was working *beautifully!*

"All the same, I wish she'd go and hang round some of the others for a change," murmured Margia as she bent over her fretsaw. "My throat's *hoarse* with shrieking."

"Cavé! Maynie's coming!" muttered Jo. "I say, I think I'll begin." And Miss Maynard was horrified to hear her say in stentorian tones, "Hand over the rest of this affair, Margia, will you? I can't get on."

"Jo!" exclaimed the Guide lieutenant. "Why are you shouting like that?"

"Was I shouting?" asked Jo innocently. "I'm awfully sorry, Miss Maynard."

"But you are still shouting!" protested Miss Maynard. "You must not do it. You know how Madame dislikes it."

Jo murmured, "sorry!" and went on with her work in silence.

Miss Maynard went her way thoroughly perplexed.

A possible solution of the mystery ocurred to her when she interviewed Matron after *Mittagessen* about some laundry that had gone amissing. Could it be possible that the girls were catching it from *her?* There would be trouble if it went on—that was certain. Miss Maynard decided to take instant steps to check it.

The first opportunity came during the evening, when the girls were wandering about the garden. Margia was surrounded by her own particular set, amongst them, Elisaveta. To the horror of the mistress the little Princess was

47

audible from the other side of the tennis-lawn. What her people would think if they could hear her, Miss Maynard was appalled to think. She fled over to the children. "Elisaveta!" she exclaimed; "you must not talk so loudly! I can hear you at the other side of the garden!"

"Can you, Miss Maynard?" said Elisaveta, wide-eyed. "I did not know I am sorry."

"It is dreadful!" declared the mathematics mistress. "If I hear you—or any other girl, for that matter! —talking so loudly, I shall give her lines for the future."

Then she turned away, leaving the wicked band chuckling over the success of their scheme. They took little notice of the mistress's warning, and before the last middle was in bed that night, four of theme were condemned to spend part of their free time on Monday in writing out Shakespeare's words twenty times in their best hand-writing.

Sunday was a little worse than Saturday. Some of the babies were beginning to pick it up, and Miss Durrant, who had charge of them that day, was nearly at her wits' end to know how to check it. To add to the difficulty, Matron had lately taken to insisting that the girls should "speak up," which from her meant "raise your voice." It really was a very awkward situation.

The climax came when the girls went out for their usual stroll up the valley to the tiny hamlet of Lauterbach. It was mid-May by this time, and the first visitors for the summer were coming. The big hotels at Buchau were beginning to open, and soon the whole peninsula would be gay with many people. This lasted for about four months, and during this time the peasants of the valley made their yearly harvest. There was little doing in the autumn and winter, and what came now had to serve most of them for the rest of the year.

Many visitors brought their children with them, and in this way the Chalet School profited, for it was easier for most of the parents to send their girls there for the morning lessons, so that they were safe. Besides this, a number of Innsbruckers came up to the Tiern See to spend the summer in their summer chalets which were built round the lake, and the girls were day-girls for the term. The Merciers were expecting their parents to come to the Kron Prinz Karl for the summer, and several of the others would join their people sooner or later, coming to school every day. Only a few of them were boarders during the summer term.

For these reasons, Miss Bettany was always careful to impress on the girls the necessity for good behaviour out of doors, and they generally were very good. To-day, however, they shrieked and talked and laughed at the tops of their voices, and, as Mademoiselle disgustedly told them, made as much noise as the peasants at carnival time.

"But it is not *gentille*," she expostulated. "You must not shout thus, but speak with gentle tones, and softly. It is not well for you to make visitors think that we of the Chalet School are rude—rough—noisy."

They stopped at once; their plan was never intended to harm their school. All the same, Mademoiselle was thankful when she had them safely behind the fence. She kept a sharp lookout on them for the rest of the day, and as they saw no reason for moderating their tones once they were away from public view, she heard enough to satisfy her that it was a general infection.

Miss Bettany listened in dismayed silence to the reports that met her when she returned from Innsbruck the next day.

"I fear, *chérie*, that it is Matron whom we must blame," wound up Mademoiselle. "Would it not be possible to send her away at the half-term?"

Madge shook her head. "Not unless we pay her salary in lieu of notice."

"Then I think we had better do so," said Mademoiselle with unexpected firmness. "I would rather spend a few pounds and rid ourselves of her, than keep her and let her spoil the whole school."

Miss Bettany said nothing. She rather thought so herself.

Mademoiselle had plenty to say on the subject, but what she was about to remark she never did, for at that moment Elisaveta passed the study door, and the two mistresses heard her say at the full pitch of healthy lungs, "I'll go and bag the whole caboodle, Joey, old peach."

Joey, shouting as if she were an irate skipper on the quarter-deck, replied, "All sereno, old fruit! Carry on, and I'll follow!"

Miss Bettany looked petrified. "How *dreadful!*" she gasped. "I must put a stop to this at once. Such language I will not allow; and as for the tones, I feel inclined to put them both in silence for the day."

She stalked over to the door, opened it, and called the pair to her.

49

They came, looking as angelic as they could.

"Did you want us, Madame?" inquired Joey in flute-like tones.

"Yes!" said her sister. "I wish to remind you both that *no* gentlewoman ever shrieks her remarks for the whole world to hear. Also that slang of most kinds is forbidden here—most certainly vulgar slang of the kind I heard you using just now."

Elisaveta looked at her with limpid pansy-brown eyes. "Is 'caboodle' slang?" she asked. "I thought it was all right; I have heard it here?"

Madge fell into the trap. "You have heard one of the girls using such a word as that?" she asked incredulously.

"Oh no, Madame," replied Elisaveta; "it wasn't a *girl*."

Miss Bettany then realised what she had done, but she merely said, "Then please do not use it again. You may both go, now; and you may write out for me what Shakespeare says is an excellent thing in woman, thirty times. Perhaps then you will realise the truth of his saying."

They went off, not noticeably damped by the punishment, and she shut the door behind them.

"You are right, Maddie," she said; "Matron must go."

CHAPTER IX

THE FINAL STRAW

MISS BETTANY having come to the momentous decision to get rid of Matron at half-term, made up her mind to speak to her in the afternoon. She was busy all the morning teaching the seniors; seeing to the re-marking of the two tennis-courts; and discussing Margia's music with Herr Anserl.

She was about to send for Matron and get the unpleasant —she knew it would be unpleasant!—interview done, when the door burst open and Princess Elisaveta, with her face scarlet and her long brown hair flying wildly, literally tumbled into the room, followed by Jo, who looked worse.

"Children!" exclaimed Miss Bettany severely. "What does this mean?"

"It's the Robin!" gasped Jo.

"She's locked her in!" Elisaveta could scarcely get the words out.

"Who has?" demanded the Head, looking as if she could have shaken the pair of them with pleasure.

"Matron has! In her room! She's crying like anything!" was the incoherent answer. "*Do* go and make her let her out!"

At this moment Miss Maynard appeared on the scene, looking angrier than anyone had ever seen Miss Maynard look.

"Matron has locked the Robin into her own room," she said in hard tones, "and refuses to open the door for me or Miss Durrant. Will you please come at once, Madame, and make her let her out at once? The child will cry herself into a fit it it lasts much longer."

Miss Bettany sped past them and up the stairs, where the few girls who happened to be in the house at the moment were clustered round the door, with shocked faces. The Robin was sobbing terribly. She was obviously quite hysterical, and Miss Bettany could hear the pitiful catches in her breath as she cried.

Matron was standing by, a key in her hand, a grimly determined expression on her face. Even when she saw the headmistress she made no attempt to move.

"The key, if you please, Matron," said Miss Bettany.

Matron held it down. "Robin has been very impertinent and troublesome," she said. "She deserves her punishment, and I must insist that you leave her to me. I cannot possibly keep order if you interfere with my punishments, Miss Bettany. I am a much older woman than you, and I have had far more experience. I must beg you to uphold my authority."

"The key, if you please," said Miss Bettany in icy tones. "As for your authority, Matron, in this school, you cease from this moment to have any. I am waiting for the key."

Matron had gone red, but there was something in the dark eyes fronting her that made her give up the key. The next minute the door was open, and the Robin was safe in the arms of her "Tante Marguerite." She was a nervous, excitable child, and the experience had completely upset

51

her. In all the seven years of her life she had never been treated like this. Miss Bettany carried her off to the study, and set to work to console her, but it was a long time before she could get the heavy sobs hushed and the child reduced to something like herself. When at length she lay on the couch, quiet at last, with only an occasional catch of her breath to show how violent the attack had been, the Head sent for a drink of water for her, and then carried her upstairs to her own room, quite worn out. She soon fell asleep on the bed, and then Miss Bettany descended the stairs, to find Joey and Elisaveta waiting for her at the bottom. "Come into the study and tell me what you know of this," she said. They followed her into the room. "What began it all?" she asked, when they were sitting down.

"Miss Wilson had forgotten her ref's whistle," explained Joey. "She had left it in our dormy this morning when she came in after games with us. I banged myself, and she came upstairs to see that I put something on the place, 'cos Matron was busy over at Le Petit Chalet. She asked the Robin to go and fetch it for her, and the babe said she would. Then Miss Wilson remembered that you had said that the little ones were not to go into the dormies at all, so she sent me after her to send her back and get the whistle myself. I was too late, though, 'cos the Robin had run, and I couldn't, 'cos my knee's rather stiff. When I got there Matron was shaking her and calling her a bad girl to break the rules like that. The Robin said she had been sent, and Matron told her not to tell lies. The kid was wild—she's a Brownie, and anyway, she never tells lies. She told Matron that she was rude not to believe her. It made Matron wild, and she shook her harder, and said she would lock her up in her cupboard to teach her to speak the truth. The Robin began to cry and said she *had* spoken the truth, and Matron lugged her along and locked her into her room, and then the Robin began to cry ever so hard. Elisaveta came along then, and we begged Matron to let her out. I said Miss Wilson had sent her, and she said, 'A likely story!'" Joey flushed darkly at this point, and the Princess took up the tale. "She was horrid to Joey, and when Miss Durrant heard us, and came and told Matron that you never let anyone be locked up, she was rude to *her*. Then Miss Maynard came and tried to make her let Robin out, and Jo and I came for you—and that's all." Elisaveta suddenly ran down and wriggled in her chair.

"I see," said Miss Bettany quietly. "Thank you, girls. That is all I want from you just now. You may go, and send the others to me."

They got up and went to the door. She called them back. "You will, of course, say nothing about the affair at present."

"Yes, Madame," replied Elisaveta.

Jo waited till she had gone, then she turned to her sister. "Did you mean what you said to Matron just now, Madge?"

"Yes; I meant it, Joey," replied Miss Bettany gently.

A tap at the door interrupted them, and Miss Bettany got up and went to tell the others that nothing was to be said to the school at large about the afternoon's occurrences until she gave them permission. "Matron will be leaving us shortly," she said. "Let that be sufficient for just now."

Miss Bettany sent for Mademoiselle, told her what had occurred, and asked her to make out a cheque for the term's salary for Matron. When that was done they sent for her, and after a most unpleasant interview sent her off to pack. It was too late for her to leave Briesau that day, but she was to go to one of the hotels for the night. Miss Bettany had decided that she should not spend another night under the roof of the Chalet School. Herr Braun, of the Kron Prinz Karl, would put her up and see her to the first train down to Spärtz in the morning, and they would be finished with her.

Miss Webb made herself as nasty as she knew how, but even she was rather subdued by the tone in the young Head's voice; and finally, she took the generous cheque they gave her and departed to her room to pack up her boxes. Eigen would go and fetch his elder brother Hans from the Kron Prinz Karl to help him carry them to the steamer in the morning; and by six o'clock—eighteen by continental time—Matron had shaken the dust of the Chalet School off her shoes, and they were rid of her.

Very little was said to the Robin that night. She was told that Matron had gone away and would not come back. Then Madge and Joey set themselves to amuse her and make her forget what had happened.

She was put to bed early, for she was still tired and unlike herself, and Madge sat beside her till she had fallen asleep. As for the S.S.M., its days were over—which was just as well. The members turned their attention to other things, and the Chalet School settled down to its old tranquillity.

CHAPTER X

ELISAVETA IS ENROLLED

"ELISAVETA, are you ready?" Joey Bettany looked excited as she came to the Princess, who stood alone behind the horse-shoe formation in which most of the others were drawn up. The only exceptions to the rule were the colour parties, which had just taken their places in front of the other Guides, and now stood like images, holding the flags. In front of the Guides stood the Brownies, very thrilled at this enrolment of a princess—the entire school knew who Elisaveta was by this time—and doing their best to look smart and workman-like.

Elisaveta, clad in blue jumper and skirt, with her yellow tie hanging loose—where the others had theirs pinned with the little metal badge that meant so much to them all—marched forward shyly at Joey's side.

Between the flags stood Miss Bettany in her captain's uniform, the other officer behind her, and, on one side, Crown Prince Carol of Belsornia, who had managed to snatch a week's holiday to come and see his little daughter enrolled. He wore his white and silver uniform as colonel of the Royal Guards, and his medals flashed in the sunlight, even though he stood, erect and still, eyes front, hand resting on his sword-hilt.

He had been overjoyed at the difference in Elisaveta when he saw her. She was rosy with long hours in the open air, simple food, quiet sleep, and jolly friends, who teased her, laughed with her, and helped her to get into mischief as often as possible. She was losing her "only-child" ways, and was becoming a thorough little school-girl. The Crown

Prince thought that the doctor could no longer complain that her vitality was being sapped away!

She came with Joey, very serious, and full of the promise she was about to make. They marched up to where Miss Bettany stood, and then Joey saluted smartly and took two steps back, standing at attention, while the captain asked the simple questions:

"Do you know what your honour is?"

"Yes." Elisaveta's reply rang out, full of confidence.

"Can I trust you on your honour to be loyal to God and the King; to help other people at all times; and to obey the Guide Law?"

Up went Elisaveta's hand to the half-salute as she replied in clear tones, "I promise on my honour to do my best to be loyal to God and the King; to help other people at all times; and to obey the Guide Law!"

"I trust you on your honour to keep this promise. You are now one of the great sister-hood of Guides." The captain's tones were very comforting. There was a quiet strength in her voice which Elisaveta found restful.

The new Guide gave her left hand in the Guide grip, and then she half-turned on the word of command and saluted the colours. Finally she saluted the company, and then she marched back to her patrol with Joey, the badge in her tie, and a deep resolve in her heart to do her best to keep her promise and to do the Guides honour by her behaviour.

Then the command rang out, "Company dismiss to patrol corners!" and it was all over.

Prince Carol smiled as Miss Bettany turned to him. "It is a splendid movement, Mademoiselle. I hope, with his Majesty's permission, to establish a branch in Belsornia. I have been reading the books you sent me very carefully, and it seems to me that it is just what is needed for our young girls."

"It is wonderful, sir," replied Madge quietly. "I am glad you think of doing so." Then she gave a short order to Miss Maynard, and the Guides gave an exhibition of company drill which impressed him very much. After the company drill, the Cock and the Poppy patrols showed the work they had done in ambulance and stretcher drill, and the Cornflowers and the Swallows gave a good display of signalling, with the Morse code.

Then it was the turn of the Brownies, and they gave a remarkable version of the work of Florence Nightingale in the Crimea, showing that they could make knots calculated to remain tied; that they knew quite a surprising amount about elementary bandaging; and signalling, slowly, of course, but quite accurately, in semaphore, with their arms.

They also treated him to a pow-wow ring, sang their verses—"There were two Sixes"—and finished up with the Brownie howl. He was delighted in it, and when it was over, and the school was racing to its dormitories to change into frocks before *Mittagessen,* he said so to the captain.

"I like your father, Elisaveta," observed Joey as she struggled into a fresh blue-linen frock. "He has a lot of sense."

"He's a dear!" said his daughter fervently.

He was! Two days after he had gone there came a huge parcel, addressed to the school, and when they opened it they found inside—twenty new books for the library, two dozen of the best tennis-balls, and thirty gramophone records.

"You've got a splendid father, Elisaveta," said Grizel Cochrane. "I do think he is the kindest man I've heard of."

"Daddy always likes doing things like that," said his daughter, colouring with pleasure at the words. Grizel was a prefect, and a very lordly person, so her condescension in saying such a thing to a mere middle, and a new girl at that, was simply amazing.

Elisaveta had been long enough at school to realise *that;* and, in any case, it was quite in keeping with all the best traditions of her beloved books.

On the tennis-court she found an agitated Margia waiting for her. "Well, you might have hurried a little!" was the young lady's greeting. "What on earth have you been doing?"

"Nothing much," replied Elisaveta. "I've been talking—that's all."

"Well, come on now, and let's get started. If we hang about much longer we shall have the big ones coming, and saying we've had the court long enough. Will you toss for service?"

Elisaveta twirled her racquet, and Margia called. As she won the call, and with it the court with the sun behind her, she soothed down, and they were soon hard at it. They were very evenly matched. Elisaveta had sometimes played with her father, and had a very swift service for a small girl; Margia had a splendid fore-hand drive, considering that she was only thirteen, but her back-hand was weak. Neither could volley, and any attempt at it always brought about disaster. The games prefect, Grizel herself, strolled over to watch them presently, and with her came Juliet Carrick, the Head's ward, and the head-girl of the school. Juliet was nearly eighteen, and was a very capable person. She had made up her mind to teach, and was working for a mathematics scholarship to the University of London. She wanted to go there, work for a science degree, and then come back and teach at the Chalet School.

Jo wandered along, and joined them after a while. "Margia is really good, isn't she?" she remarked.

Juliet nodded. "She is shaping very well," she said. "That new child, Elisaveta, is going to be good, too. She hasn't anything like Margia's strength, of course, but she's got a very decent service already. Margia's drives are something out of the common for a kiddie of her age."

"She says it's all the practise she does," said Joey. "She says her arm-muscles are so developed that she can hit harder than most people."

"Her back-hand strokes are frightfully weak, though," put in Grizel. "Look at that attempt! 'Rotten' simply doesn't describe it!"

"No wonder, when you notice the way she holds her racquet!" said Juliet. "The wonder is she can do anything with it. What's the score, anyone?"

Elisaveta answered her as Margia missed a return on to the back line. "Forty—thirty! Send that ball back, Margia, will you, please? I have only one at this side."

"The hopes of their side," said Joey with a grin. "Isn't it a pity we can't play against any other schools?"

"It is—rather," said Juliet. "There! That's game to Elisaveta. Hop across and tell Margia about holding her racquet properly, Grizel."

Grizel strolled across the court, and proceeded to give a lecture on how to hold one's racquet for the back-hand drive, illustrating with wide sweeps of Margia's racquet.

The tennis match went on between the two, but Joey marched off into the house. There she encountered her sister, who was holding an open letter in her hand, and looking more disturbed than Joey had ever seen her before. "Madge! What's the matter?" she asked in startled tones.

Miss Bettany looked at her abstractedly. "I wish you

wouldn't use my name like that, Joey," she said. "Anyone might hear you."

"There isn't anyone to hear," replied Jo, slipping her hand through her sister's arm. "What is the matter, old thing?"

"It's nothing you can help, Joey."

"You never know. Don't shut me out, Madge; we've always shared things."

"I know." Miss Bettany looked at the clever, sensitive face at her shoulder. "Sometimes I think, Joey, that we've put too much on you. I don't want to spoil your childhood."

"It won't spoil my anything to share your fusses. There's only us—and the Robin. Dick seems so far away since he married Mollie. *You're* going to get married next. I—I hope it won't be like that."

Madge pulled the child into the study. "Joey-Baba, you don't really think that? Jem will only be like an extra brother. It's different with Dick and Mollie. We've never seen her; we don't really know her. Don't think of it like that, Joey, or I must put off the wedding till you are grown-up!"

Joey flung her arms round her sister in a tempestuous hug. "I'm a *beast* to say such things! I know it'll be all right! Jem is a dear, and I hope you will be married soon! So don't be silly, old thing!"

Madge still looked troubled. "Truth and honour, Joey?"

"Truth and honour," Joey assured her. "I didn't really mean it, and I only think it *very* rarely. Honour bright, I do!"

Madge's face cleared. "I am glad of that, Joey," she said slowly. "You see this is the last term. Jem and I hope to be married in July."

Joey looked at her; then she gulped hard. "T-tell me what is wrong with your letter," she said huskily.

Madge answered hurriedly, "It is from Prince Carol, Joey. He writes to tell me that he is afraid that his cousin, Cosimo, may make an attempt to kidnap the Princess. He has quarrelled with the King, and Prince Carol as well, and he made some threat of the kind once before when they had a difference. He does not know where she is—no one in Belsornia except them, her maid, Alette, and Dr Tracy do. But he is afraid he may find out, and then, if he does, Elisaveta must be taken somewhere into safe hiding until the trouble is over. He warns me not to let her speak to any strangers. If ever you see any attempt to speak to her, Joey, you must stop it somehow. They don't want her to know anything about it, as he is afraid of making her nervous. Don't say anything, but just watch."

"I'll stick to her like glue," promised Joey. "But I say, Madge, it's rather awful, isn't it? What would he do to her if he got her away? Kill her?"

"Nonsense, Joey! Don't let your imagination run away with you like that! The worst thing he would do would be to hold her as a hostage while he made the King and the Prince do as he wanted. But he wouldn't hurt her. He would get into all sorts of trouble if he did that."

"I see," said Joey thoughtfully. "Well, I'll do my best. She's awfully jolly, isn't she? It is hard luck that she can't be Queen some day!"

"They have the Salic law in Belsornia," replied Madge. "I don't know that it is such a pity, Joey. I don't think a queen's is such an enviable existence. I wish I knew what would be the best thing to do," she went on, more to herself than her sister. "So long as he doesn't know where she is, she's pretty safe. But I think I'll ask him to send someone to whom I could apply if there was any difficulty."

Joey looked solemn. "Do you think he *is* likely to kidnap her, Madge?"

"Goodness knows! I don't see how he can find out where she is, because she came like any other new pupil, and certainly no one is making any extra fuss over her. But it's rather a big responsibility. I don't know that I should have taken her if I had dreamt there would be any trouble like this!"

"Oh, well! We don't know that he'll try to cart her off," said Jo easily; "and we can keep a firm eye on her—I will, myself, if it's any comfort to you."

"I accept your offer," returned her sister. "What about a game of tennis, if we can get two other people to make up a set?"

"Rather! Come on!" And, troubles all forgotten for the moment, they made their way to the tennis-courts for a strenuous set.

CHAPTER XI

UP THE ZILLERTHAL

"JOEY—Joey Bettany!"

Back came the answer. "Hello! What do you want?"

"Where are you?" called Grizel.

"Up in the pine-tree just behind you. Look out! I'm coming." There was a scramble and a clatter, and then Joey tumbled out of the pine almost on the top of Grizel.

"What on earth were you doing up there?" demanded the games prefect. "Madame wants you at once. Buck along. She's in the study."

"What on earth does she want now?" grumbled Joey, who had just got comfortably settled with her book, and resented having to leave her perch.

"I didn't ask her," replied Grizel. "If you go, you'll soon find out."

"Suppose you go instead of me," suggested Jo.

"Is that intended for a joke?" demanded Grizel. "If so, it's a rotten one."

Joey grinned. "I'd enjoy seeing her face if you *did* go and say you'd come instead of me!" she said, as she turned towards the house. "*Wouldn't* there be a fuss?"

She was out of hearing by the time Grizel thought of a sufficiently squelching answer, so that young lady let it go, and went off to the lake where the other prefects were waiting for her before they rowed over to Buchau on the other shore. Joey, meanwhile, trotted off to the study, where she found her sister sitting on the window-ledge, looking out. She turned her head as the younger girl entered the room. "There you are," she said. "I've sent for you to see if you know what the girls would like to do on the fourth."

"Why, it's not for a fortnight!" said Jo in amazement.

"You *are* in a hurry for your birthday to come this year! Where's the rush?"

"It's the last birthday I shall have as Head of the school," explained her sister. "I want it to be extra nice—that's all."

"Oh, I see!" Joey squeezed herself into the narrow space left by her sister, and considered the matter gravely. "I don't think there's anything special they want to do."

"Sure?"

"Yes—absolutely certain. Why? Have you got an idea of your own, then?"

"Well, I rather thought of a day at Mayrhofen in the Zillerthal."

Joey's black eyes widened with excitement. *"Madge!* What a gorgeous idea! I loved the Zillerthal when we were there last summer, and I should think most people would go crazy over it! It's nearly as nice as Briesau—only it hasn't got the lake, of course."

"You really think the others would like it?"

"They'd be idiots if they didn't! *Do* fix on it straight away!"

Miss Bettany laughed. "You *are* enthusiastic! Well, it seems to me about the best thing we can do. If it's fine, then, we'll go there. If it's wet, I'll take you all down to Hall, and we'll do it thoroughly."

"I hope it's fine," said Joey sincerely. "Are you going to tell the others now?' '

"No. I'm going to leave Juliet to do that," replied Madge. "She will like it, and it's *her* last term, too—as head-girl."

"I *hate* coming to the end of things!" said Jo vigorously.

"Most of us do. Run along and tell Juliet that I want her."

Joey slid down from her precarious perch, and ran out of the room to the lake, where Juliet was in a boat with the others—luckily, not far from the shore. "Ju-li-*et!*" Joey's golden voice rang out over the water, and Juliet turned her head with its masses of long, fair hair. "Yes?" she called.

"Madame wants you."

"All right; I'm coming."

The boat was turned, and Juliet sprang to land; while Joey, having delivered her message, sauntered off to the woods, where she presently encountered Elisaveta. With her was Simone Lecoutier, who, in the early days of the

61

school, had had a craze for Joey. Two years had made a difference, and the sentimental French child had learned to understand that Joey could be friendly with her and two or three other people as well. There had been a good many scenes before Simone had been persuaded to realise this; but at last she did, and they were far better friends than they had ever been before. Joey said that Simone had learnt a little common-sense. At any rate, she no longer insisted that they two should be all in all to each other, much to Jo's relief.

Elisaveta ran up to her friend when she saw her. "Joey," she cried, "I've an idea! Couldn't we ask the visitors to play us at tennis,"

Jo shook her head. "I don't quite see how we could. Of course, some of them come every year, and we know them —more or less, that is. But I'm sure my sister wouldn't agree to asking any of them to play a match with us like that. You can't do that sort of thing in a school. We have the inter-form matches anyhow, so I don't see what you are all grumbling at!"

"But it *wasn't* grumbling," protested Elisaveta. "It was only meant to be an idea."

"Oh, well, it's no good anyway," replied Joey, slipping her arm through Simone's. "Come on, you two. I've got a gorgeous piece of news which I can't tell you——"

"But why, then, speak of it?" demanded Simone. "It is unkind, Jo."

"No, it isn't! It's only sort of giving you an appetite for it when it comes."

Simone shook her head over this; but there was no arguing with Jo, and they had to possess their souls in patience till *Kaffee*, when Juliet rose with much dignity and announce the Head's scheme for her birthday.

It was greeted with shouts of joy, and from that minute the girls could talk of little else.

The Head had asked the girls to give her no birthday gift this year. Her real reason was that she was leaving them at the end of the term, as all the parents knew, and she preferred that they should omit the practice which had held good for the other two fête-days. The girls, of course, knew nothing about it, and were not to know until after the trip to the Zillerthal. Miss Bettany did not want them upset any sooner, though she felt that it would not be fair to them to slip away without letting them know till it was all over, which had been her first plan. The school had appeared to fall in with her wishes, but in reality they had decided to get something for the school, and already Herr Marani had been commisioned to choose two pictures, and have them sent up to Herr Braun of the Kron Prinz Karl, so that they might be safely kept until the birthday morning.

"We won't say anything to Joey," declared Juliet. "She would probably let it out to Madame, and then she'd stop it. It won't really matter, because Jo is sure to have her own present."

So Jo knew nothing but that the usual presentation of flowers would take place, and she joined the serenading party quite cheerfully on the morning of the fourth, having slipped into her sister's room and laid her own gift on the table at the bedside.

They sang "Hark, Hark, the Lark" to Schubert's lovely setting, and, as they finished, Miss Bettany thrust out a ruffled head to look down on them, as they stood beneath her window, and thank them.

"We've got another one," called Juliet.

The Head pulled her dressing-gown round her more closely, and settled herself to listen. It was a very simple little song that greeted her surprised ears, and was a verse —one only; Joey hadn't been able to manage any more!— on her name:

I sing the charms of Margaret, sweet and kind,
   No fairer maiden ever graced this day;
The richest pearl she is that man could find.
   It is thy birth-morn! Sweeting, come away.

Miss Bettany listened to this in startled silence. The air was as simple as the words, but with a certain freshness which covered one or two rather glaring mistakes in composition. When it was over, she leaned out of the window. "Where did you get that?" she demanded.

Juliet answered her. "Joey wrote the words, and Margia the tune," she called.

"Good gracious!" The Head nearly fell out in her surprise.

"Do you like it?" called the small sister of the composer.

"Yes; very, very much indeed! It's the most charming thing I ever heard!" Miss Bettany suddenly felt a big lump in her throat, and was unable to go on. She drew back into the room to recover herself; and the girls, well pleased with themselves, went off to their duties. Jo was the only

63

one who left them neglected, and she fled upstairs to wish her sister many happy returns. She found her sitting on the bed, scrubbing her eyes with her handkerchief.

"Many - happy - returns - what - on-earth - is - the - matter?" panted Jo, all in one breath.

"I'm an idiot! " replied Madge, with a little choke. "It was so unexpected that I felt all choky—that's all."

"I see. D'you like my present?" asked Jo, turning the conversation at once.

"I haven't looked at it yet. Give it to me, Joey."

Joey passed it over to her, and then stood by while Madge peeled off the many outer wrappings, and finally disclosed to view—six teaspoons! !

"Awfully appropriate, isn't it?" said Jo complacently. "They aren't real silver, of course. I thought they'd do for everyday ones."

"They are awfully startling," said Madge faintly. "I never expected such a thing."

"We—ll, they aren't silver at all," confessed Joey. "They only cost a very little. You see, I'm saving up for your wedding present."

A tap on the door prevented her sister from replying to this, and the Robin entered, hugging a big bundle. Jo had helped her choose, and this turned out to be a pudding-basin!

"It will be useful, Ma Tante, I think," said the baby wistfully. "You like it?"

"It's a *splendid* present!" said the recipent as she gave the small person a hug and a kiss. "They are both most useful; and thank you both very much."

Then she sent them away to see to their beds, and lay back on her pillows and laughed till her sides ached.

After *Frühstück* they all scattered to make their beds, and then prayers came, and with them the presentation of the flowers, a thing which was never omitted. Madge Bettany stood there on the little dais, half-smiling, half-serious, for this was the last time that the little ceremony would take place. She expected to spend her next birthday on the Sonnalpe, with Dr Jem. Joey, who knew this too, felt choky. "I wish there need never be any changes," she thought to herself as she wriggled restlessly in her place.

The flowers were taken up to the dais; and when they were all heaped round the Head there was a little stir, and then the Robin and little Inga Erikson, the two youngest children in the school, came up to her, each carrying a big, flat parcel.

"It is for you from the school, Madame," said Inga shyly.

Miss Bettany flushed. "But, my dears, I thought you had quite put the idea out of your heads," she said. "It is very, very kind of you, and I can't tell you how much I appreciate the thought." She finished tearing the wrappings off the first one, and showed a charming copy of "June in the Austrian Tyrol." The other was another view of the Tyrol by the same artist. "Two of my favourite pictures," she said softly. "They are beautiful! Thank you all very much indeed." Then she dismissed them to get ready for the trip, while she carried her new possessions to the study, where she pulled herself together.

Of what was to come she said nothing, of course; but all the girls said that although Madame was always sweet, she had never been so sweet as on this day. They went down to Spärtz by the funny little mountain train which crawls up the side of the mountain from the plain below to the great Tiernthal. With her were the seniors; Miss Maynard and Miss Carthew had the middles; and Mademoiselle, Miss Durrant, and Miss Wilson looked after the babies.

Marie and Eigen had come to help carry the baskets, and they were as excited as the rest. Never in all their lives had they been farther than Spärtz, and the thought of going in the train up the Zillerthal was in itself alone an adventure. That they should also go to Mayrhofen and see the pine-woods, where the Ziller dashes along from its mountain home to join the Inn, seemed to them to be too good to be true. They sat in awed silence at first, but gradually their tongues were loosened, and they chattered eagerly about the beauties of the journey. From Spärtz the Zillerthal winds its way by the banks of the river into the heart of great mountains, where the highest are covered with snow all the year round. Past beautiful woods the train wound by farm-houses, the walls of which were adorned with wonderful frescoes, and from which linty-locked children appeared to watch the train as it went past. They stopped at primitive little stations, Fugen and Ried and Zell-am-Ziller, where the railway branches off to the east, and so, at last, to Mayrhofen.

It was nearly twelve o'clock by the time they got there, so the first thing to do was to get to the woods and have

Mittagessen. They set off through the little village, where there is one *Gasthof* and two or three *Pensions,* the inhabitants of which stared at them as they "crocodiled"—the verb is Joey's—along to the woods which clothe the lower part of the Ziller Alps. Here they found not only pine-trees, but birches and mountain-ash. It was an easy matter to choose a place for their picnic, and they soon found a little clearing, where they sat down, the mistresses on a fallen log and the girls on their rain-coats, which they had brought with them. Storms come up so quickly and suddenly in these long, narrow valleys that the Head had insisted on their bringing something to protect them in case of need. She had never forgotten the awful thunderstorm which had broken during the afternoon on the occasion of her first birthday in the Tyrol. They had been up on the Mondscheinspitze, and they had had to take refuge in the herdsman's hut for the night, as the rain only cleared off late at night, and she had had no mind to essay the scramble down over tree-roots and boulders in the dark. It had been an adventure, but, as she had said at the time, one of that kind was quite enough.

It was a gorgeous feast. There were rolls, buttered, and with hard-boiled eggs beaten up with butter and cream, and shredded lettuce, in a way of which Marie alone knew the secret, slipped in. There were delicious little cakes, contributed by Dr Jem, who had brought them on the previous evening from Vienna, where he had been attending a congress of doctors, besides those which Herr Mensch had brought from his wife in Innsbruck. There were French chocolates and bonbons, there were piles of apricots and plums and greengages, and there were two huge melons. They all ate till they had had enough, and then the baskets, which were of a folding variety, were filled with what was left, the few which were empty being folded up again and tucked into one of the full ones, and then they were taken to the post-office, where the post-mistress, a cousin of Frau Pfeifen, mother of Marie and Eigen, volunteered to look after them, while they all scrambled about the lower slopes of the mountain.

"What is the best train to get back?" inquired Miss Bettany.

Frau Heiliggert looked wise. "The train back to Seespitz leaves at eighteen, mein Fraülein," she said. "It will be well to be here at ten minutes before that time. Thus there will

66

be no hurry. Marie and Eigen will stay with me, *nicht wahr?*"

They said they would, so Miss Bettany left them there and went back to her girls, who were awaiting her impatiently. They wanted to get off to the woods.

CHAPTER XII

THE TWO STRANGE MEN

HAVING got rid of all the burdens, and also left Marie and Eigen in safe hands, Miss Bettany now felt that she might enjoy herself without any cares for the next few hours. She was glad to think that the two Tyroleans were happy with their distant cousin. She knew that they were inclined to be overawed by the whole school, although they got on well enough when there were only two or three of the girls there. This was a much better arrangement.

The girls streamed away to the woods, determined to make the most of their holiday. Some of them joined the Head and chattered eagerly in a mixture of tongues to her as they strolled along in the shade of the trees; some of them raced on with the two junior mistresses; the prefects attached themselves to Mademoiselle and Miss Maynard, who found plenty to talk about; the remainder, among whom were Jo and Elisaveta, strayed off by themselves. There was a little fear of their being lost, for they had decided to keep to the banks of the river and see where it led them.

"It's a gorgeous day," said the Princess as she wandered along with Joey, who was inclined to be silent. "Isn't this a *magnificent* place? I do believe I almost like it better than the Tiern See."

"Do you? *I* don't!" said Joey, aroused from her thinking by this. "It's awfully jolly, of course; but the Tiern See is

67

simply lovely, all times! You should see it in the winter when the lake is frozen over! Now this is lovely *now*, but it won't be nearly as pretty when the winter comes. Half its beauty is the river dashing along like that. When it's frozen it will be quite different."

"Yes, I suppose so," replied Elisaveta doubtfully. "And anyway, our school's at the Tiern See, and that makes a huge difference."

Joey looked at her doubtfully. She was half-minded to tell her what was coming to the school. Then she remembered that Madge had said that nothing was to be mentioned until after the birthday, so she said instead, "Let's climb down to the water, shall we?"

Elisaveta was quite agreeable, so they scrambled down the steep, rock-strewn bank to where the water rushed along with a great deal of noise, and leaping up the stones in its bed. The children were thirsty, so they stooped down and cupped some in their hands. It was deliciously cold, as well it might be, for it came from the mountain snows, and it had a sweet taste which they had not tasted before. Of course they splashed themselves, but that was half the fun.

When they had drunk as much as they wanted, they climbed back just in time to avoid being caught by Miss Maynard, who was walking along with Juliet, Grizel, and Rosalie Dene, another of the seniors, a quiet girl, who never had much to say, but enjoyed herself in her own way.

"Where have you two been?" asked Miss Maynard as they joined her. "Don't get lost, whatever you do! Where are the others?"

"In front, I think," replied Joey.

"Run on and tell them not to get too far in advance. We don't want to lose the last train; and if they get too far away, it may take some time to fetch them back," said the mistress.

Joey and Elisaveta trotted off, and soon were shouting, "Coo-eee!" at the top of their voices. They managed to catch the girls in front, which was just as well, as they were well ahead. When the two messengers got up to them they were near the tunnel cut out of the rock where the banks deepen to a little gorge, and a plank crosses the river at a height of some thirty feet or more. Here the girls hung over the hand-rail, gazing at the water as it fought its way down to the valleys of the Lower Zillerthal. It is only a small river, but here it gives a good imitation of rapids, and the girls were fascinated by it.

Presently the others came up to them, and, when they had all their own fill of gazing, they moved on. The banks grew lower farther up the valley, and at length they came out to where it is possible to cross again by the stones in the bed. It is very shallow here, but it goes at a great rate. On the farther side there is a farm, and here they crossed and went to buy milk, which they had to drink out of a huge pan, taking it in turns to drink.

"We can stay here for about half-an-hour," said Miss Bettany, after consulting her watch. "Don't go too far away, girls, as we must be going back then. You must have *Kaffee*, and we do *not* want to spend the night here—nor have to walk back."

They scattered, after promising to return in the time, and she settled herself with the seniors, who one and all elected to stay with her. It was a hot afternoon, and they wanted to rest before going back.

The juniors were quite happy to amuse themselves in the farm-yard, and pestered the good-natured Frau with questions about all the animals and the work generally. Some of the middles took off their shoes and stockings and tried paddling in the water; but they soon gave it up—it was too stony to be pleasant. Joey and Frieda sauntered off up the river, anxious to see as much of it as they could. Elisaveta and Simone crossed back to the other bank and wandered along in the other direction. They were presently joined by Margia, who had great ideas of finding gold in the water. Her only reason for this was that it looked like the kind of river that might have gold in it!

Simone was delighted to help with the experiments; but Elisaveta soon tired of messing about in the water, and went off by herself, leaving them to get joyously wet and untidy, while she strolled away, full of her own thoughts.

She never noticed how far she was getting from everyone, and it was quite a shock to her when she heard footsteps, and, on looking up, saw a tall dark man approaching her with a smile, while no one she knew was in sight.

The stranger seemed to be anxious to prevent her from feeling alarmed, for, before she could open her mouth to call, he spoke, making a low bow. "Pardon, madame," he said. "It is our little Princess, is it not?"

Elisaveta stood upright, a little air of dignity about her. "Who are you?" she asked gravely.

"Maurús Ternikai, at your service, Highness," he replied.

"How do you know who I am?" demanded the Princess doubtfully.

"All good Belsornians know the Little Lady of Belsornia," he said, giving her the title her grandfather's people had bestowed on her when she had driven through the streets to be christened in the great cathedral of Firarto, the capital of Belsornia.

She knew by this that he must be a Belsornian, so she smiled at him. "What does a Belsornian do in a strange country?" she asked.

"He watches over the Little Lady, madame," he replied.

Elisaveta stared. "Why?" she asked quickly.

He bowed again. "I trust the Gracious One will not be angry with her servant," he said humbly. "It is necessary, Highness; it is very necessary. There are dangers for all of a royal house in Europe in these times. It is necessary that you should be guarded, Highness. It is the wish of his Highness the Crown Prince."

"He never told me," said the Princess quickly.

"Yet it is his wish, Highness," replied the man inflexibly. "I am obeying my orders, Highness, and I may not leave you till you are safely with those who ought to regard you as a precious and a sacred charge, and not leave you to walk here by yourself."

"Oh, for that! I came of my own wish," said the Princess indifferently.

It was odd what a change had come over her. The jolly natural child they all knew at the Chalet School had vanished, and in her place was the Princess Elisaveta of Belsornia, who had been in danger of losing all her childhood.

The man bowed profoundly again. "That may be true; yet, Highness, *it is not safe.*"

The Princess raised her eyebrows. "I do not understand you," she said. "I am perfectly safe here. There is no one but the school here, and the farm people. I thank you, signor, for your thought for me, but I am quite all right."

"It may be so. At least, Highness, you will know me now, and may be assured that I will do all in my power to save you any annoyance or trouble."

"That will be best done if you do not follow me," replied

the Princess. "I am safe with Miss Bettany, I assure you, and I need no watchfulness but hers."

"The Signorina Bettany knows that I am to come," said the man. "It is her own wish that I should be here, Highness. She will tell you that herself. It is her request to his Highness that has helped to bring me so soon."

Elisaveta bent her head. "If my father has sent you, I cannot do anything but obey his wishes," she said. "I thank you, signor. I will now return to the others, as we shall soon be going back to the Tiern See."

Again she made that curiously stately little bend of the head and, turning, walked away from him.

He looked after her with a smile which was strangely triumphant. "The first step has been taken," he muttered to himself. "Who would have thought it would have been so easy? She even told me where she is without any questions on my part. The Prince should reward me well for this."

Elisaveta walked sedately along till she reached the place where Margia and Simone had been carrying on their gold-washing operations. They were there no longer, and that told her that she had been away longer than she had intended. At that thought she flung her royal dignity to the winds and took to her heels. She got up to the stepping-stones panting and breathless, and found that all the others had just gathered there, and they were calling her and Joey and Frieda, who came racing along from the other direction.

"You sinful children!" said Miss Bettany laughingly. "You are late, the three of you!"

She had not seen which way Elisaveta had come, and took it for granted that she had been with the other two.

"Where *did* you get to?" demanded Margia of the Princess as they walked rapidly back. "We couldn't see you anywhere."

"I went along the stream a little way," replied Elisaveta. She said nothing about her meeting with Maurús Ternikai, because it never entered her head to do so. Margia was not a special friend of hers, and she could see no reason why she should mention anything so private as the sudden appearance of a bodyguard for her—especially as he had said that Miss Bettany had asked for one for her. Elisaveta thought that she might perhaps tell Joey about it, but no

71

one else. She felt a great liking for the Head's sister, but Margia was not the type of child to appeal to her.

Joey, however, was interested in Frieda's plans for the summer holidays. She kept with her, and Elisaveta had no chance of telling her new friend anything as long as they were in the woods.

When they were all sitting down to *Kaffee* and *Kuchen*, however, in the garden of the *Gasthaus*, Jo pulled the Princess into a seat by her. "Where did you go this afternoon?" she asked in a friendly manner. "I never saw you till you came flying back along the path. I thought you were with Margia and Simone. You mustn't go off by yourself! Why didn't you come with us if you didn't want to stick with them?"

"They were trying to find gold in the river," explained Elisaveta. "I thought it was a stupid game, so I left them and went on a little way."

"Gold in the river?" Joey was wide-eyed. "What on earth made them think of that?"

"Margia said it looked like a river to have gold in," replied the Princess in rather a muddled fashion. "Joey! Sit with me when we go back, will you? I want to tell you something."

"Righto!" agreed Jo cheerfully. "We'll try to get a corner to ourselves."

But when they did get the corner to themselves and she had heard Elisaveta's story, she looked serious. "I say! Have you told my sister?"

Elisaveta shook her head. "No; if she asked for him to be sent, she will know all about it, and she might not like to be worried about it. People *don't* talk of such things, you know."

Joey didn't know, but she thought Elisaveta probably did, so she said nothing more, and the conversation turned on school subjects till they reached Spärtz and were getting into the little mountain train to go up to Seespitz. Then Elisaveta touched her arm. "Look, Joey! That man there! That is he!"

Joey looked. "Is it? He's got someone with him. See, Elisaveta! They evidently don't want you to notice them, 'cos they're hiding behind that luggage. How funny!"

Elisaveta wrinkled up her brow thoughtfully. "I know that other man," she said. "I can't think who he is, but I know him quite well, I'm sure."

What Joey would have had to say on the subject was lost, for at that moment Grizel, Juliet, and the Robin joined them, and there was no further chance of private talk that night.

CHAPTER XIII

SOME STARTLING NEWS

AFTERWARDS, when everything was over and done with, someone asked the two girls why they had said nothing about the meeting and the two men's behaviour on the station-platform at Spärtz. Joey's reply that they hadn't really thought it worth mentioning, since she knew that her sister expected a kind of bodyguard for the Princess, while Elisaveta knew that royalty has to submit to precautions of this kind, seemed to them to account for things quite satisfactorily. Their questioner, who was no less a person than the King of Belsornia himself, smiled. "As things have turned out," he said, "no real harm has come of it. But when there are unusual happenings, and you know that none of the elders know of them, it is generally better to mention them to someone in charge."

All that, however, came much later. At the time neither of the children said anything about it on the day it occurred, and the next day saw them all too busy preparing for the Guide tests, which came on the Saturday, to think of anything outside of Guides.

Joey was to make an effort to get her Needlewoman's badge. She had tried for it three times already, but her sewing hadn't been up to standard the first time; the second time her mending had let her down. This time she had made a big effort, and her garment had passed muster with Frau Marani, who was examiner for the test, and now she had only her patch and darning to do, and the cutting out and button-holes and seeing of gathers into a band to get through.

Elisaveta was taking ambulance and child-nurse, and she wandered about distractedly, murmuring the names of the principal bones to herself till she finally made an idiot of herself, as Joey said, by replying, when Miss Wilson asked her where the Carpathians were, "Oh, they are the bones that are in the hand!!"

Her agitated explanation, made after Miss Wilson had finished telling her what she thought of her, that "metacarpal" was not *very* unlike "Carpathians," brought her no satisfaction.

It seemed to the excited children as if the day would never end. When, at last, *Kaffee* brought to a close the school-hours, there was a general sigh of relief to be heard from the various classes. Even the seniors were not above that.

"Thank goodness! No more lessons till Monday!" exclaimed Juliet Carrick in the privacy of the prefects' room, where she was putting away her possessions. "I feel as if this term would *never* end!"

"I feel rather that way too," acknowledged Grizel. "There's a sort of *waiting* feeling in the air—you know what I mean?"

Juliet nodded. "I do! I feel it myself. I don't know what it is, but it's a restless sensation. I wonder if Madame is going to spring something on us."

"Such as what?" demanded Bette Rincini, a very pretty Tyrolean, who was one of the original pupils of the school. Bette had learned to speak English almost perfectly, and her use of English slang was a source of mystery to her companions, who would never understand how it was that she never made mistakes.

Grizel looked across at her now and laughed. "I don't know; and I'm sure that Juliet can't say either. P'r'aps we're going to have a new building erected."

"I hope not!!" Bette was quite decided on that point. "I should hate to leave the Chalet! I've always been so glad that it was the babies who were sent to Le Petit Chalet, and not we!"

"So have I," said Juliet, leaving her locker and coming over to the window where the other two were standing. "I don't think it's *that* though, Bette, so you needn't get worried over that."

74

"Then what *do* you think it is?" demanded Grizel.

Juliet shook her head. "Don't know, I'm sure—*Herein!*" as a tap sounded at the door.

The Robin appeared in reply, with an air of deep mystery on her face. "Juliette, will you come to Madame *now*, please? She wants you."

"The solution to the mystery!!" Grizel called after her as she went.

"More than likely!" retorted the head-girl, taking the Robin's hand. "Come along, Robin."

"We're going to have tea with Madame," the baby informed her as they walked to the study. "It's a lovely tea, with *English* tea, and cakes!"

"Who're 'we'?" asked Juliet.

"You, an' me, an' Joey!" The Robin had just got over her difficulty with English "J's," and was very proud of herself. She still made mistakes if she was excited or in a hurry, but she remembered in time now.

"How fabulous!" said Juliet.

By this time they had reached the door, and there was Miss Bettany, waiting for them, with Joey standing beside her.

"Come along, girls," she said. "We are going to take our tea to the pines, as the others are to have *Kaffee* in the garden. Juliet, take that basket, dear, and Robin can carry this one. Now, come along!"

They set out, Joey bearing the thermos flasks, and the Head herself with the basket containing milk and cakes. The others saw them going.

"Tea with Madame!" exclaimed Bette. "Well, there's nothing to be gained there, then. It must be imagination!"

"What *are* you talking about!" demanded Grizel. "Of all the mixed sentences that is the worst I've ever heard. What do you mean?"

"Our feelings," replied Bette vaguely.

"Oh, I see! Well, Juliet is Madame's ward, and the Robin is something of the same kind I suppose, and Joey is her sister. They like to be together I know, and they very seldom are. There's Rosalie. Let's join her!"

The three who had gone with the Head were seen no more that night. The Robin was always sent to bed very early, as she was delicate and needed a good deal of rest. Juliet vanished out of sight, and was only found when the others went to bed, already between the sheets. Her cubicle curtains were tightly drawn, and when Grizel would have opened them to ask where she had been she was sternly ordered to "Go away, for goodness' sake, and leave me in peace." Much wondering, she did as she was told, for Juliet's tone warned her that there was to be no trifling.

As for Jo, she was in the study, helping her sister to turn out a drawer that needed it badly! She was sent to bed too, for, like the Robin, she was not a robust child, and the long day of the picnic had tired her. Also, she was rather excited by what her sister had told the three of them, even though she had known part of it before.

The next day brought the tests, and the girls all turned up to breakfast, looking especially neat and trim, with their uniforms very smart and all their accoutrements polished to the last degree.

"Thank goodness it will soon be over now!" sighed Margia, who was taking Naturalist badge and was very nervous in consequence. She was an unobservant young person, and this test had meant hard work for her.

"It's far worse to have to play to Herr Anserl!" declared Frieda, who was going in for Musician's.

Frieda played the harp, and her own master, a man from Innsbruck, was gentle in the extreme, willing to go over and over the work till his pupils saw their faults, and never losing either patience or temper. Herr Anserl frequently lost both. *Frühstück* over, however, the girls fled to the school-rooms to be sure that everything was ready, and then went off to their morning tasks before returning to the big school-room for prayers. Once prayers were over, they were settled at their tests and there was quietness in the school until half-past twelve saw the end of the morning's work, and they ran out into the garden for a rest before *Mittagessen*.

"What was the matter last night?" demanded Grizel of the head-girl, as the latter joined them. "Was anything wrong?"

"No," said Juliet briefly. "What did you think of the Health test, anyone?"

Several people had taken the test, and there was an instant chorus of answers. The general opinion was that Dr Jem who was responsible for it, had gone out of his way to make the questions unpleasant. In the chatter over it Grizel's question was forgotten, and the tests discussion lasted them through the break and the meal as well. After

Mittagessen, as it was a hot day, they all went to lie down for an hour before beginning work again. The tests were always finished within the one day, and it meant that that day was pretty well occupied. At half-past two those who had not yet finished went back to the school-rooms, and the others lazed about the garden with books and work and puzzles.

Joey and Juliet both had tests in the afternoon, and it was late before they were finished. The Head appeared at *Kaffee,* and informed them all that she was going to let them go bathing later on.

"It has been so hot to-day," she said, "that the water ought to be just right. You can all get undressed in half-an-hour's time and be ready to go in by six o'clock to-night."

"Little ones may stay up till seven o'clock to-night."

There was a buzz of joyful chatter when she had gone, for they all loved bathing in the evening, and it was not often allowed. The Tiern See is partly fed by springs in its bed, and they tend to keep it very cold. Miss Bettany was always rather afraid of cramp from this, and preferred that they should bathe during the day when the sun was on the water.

They were all at the meeting-place at the time she had named, and they went joyfully down to the lake, talking and laughing all the time. Nearly every one could swim, even the Robin being able to manage breast-stroke.

They all frolicked about—splashing each other, surface-diving, and having races. The small ones were sent in very soon, and trotted off quite happily to *Abendessen* and bed, while the others sported about for a while longer. The water was beautifully warm, and they were very reluctant to leave it when Miss Durrant blew her whistle. They soon dressed, and then sauntered out into the garden.

Abendessen was ready shortly, and when it was over there was only a short time left to the middles. They were to go to bed early, as they had had such a full day.

When the staff had taken their departure Juliet turned to the other prefects. "Get the girls together," she said. "I have something to tell them."

Grizel shot a glance at her. "Mystery?" she said.

Juliet shook her head. "You'll hear in a minute," she replied curtly.

There was a round up, and presently the school—with

77

the exception of the juniors—was gathered together on the lawn.

"Sit down," said Juliet. "I've something to tell you."

Joey, who had arrived with the rest, suddenly looked wise, but she sat down in silence—an example followed by the others. What *was* Juliet going to say to them?"

The head-girl wasted no time in beating about the bush. "I've asked you to come here," she began, "to tell you that Madame wishes you to know that she is going to be married at the end of July."

There was a startled gasp. The girls had known that the wedding would take place some time soon, but they had not expected it yet. The news that the date was fixed came as a shock to them.

Grizel recovered herself first. "So *that's* the mystery?" she said. "Well, we might have guessed it if we had thought!"

"Madame married?" cried Margia. "Oh, how *awful!*"

"*Schrecklich!*"—"*Effrayant!*"—Ghastly!" The exclamations went the round. The girls had never thought of this.

"What on earth does she want to get married for yet?" demanded Evadne in a somewhat querulous tone.

"Well, they've been engaged more than a year," Grizel reminded her.

"But won't she teach in the school any more?" Frieda sounded aghast. "Why, it won't *be* the Chalet School without Madame!"

"Where will they live, Joey?" Margia turned to Jo as being the one likely to know most about the matter.

"They'll live in the new chalet Jem has had built above the Sonnalpe," replied Jo gloomily.

"*Won't* she teach us any more, then?"

"With a house to look after?" Joey spoke in her most sarcastic tones. "Don't be silly!"

Margia retired crushed, and Frieda took up the tale. "Did Madame say *when,* Juliet?"

"Yes. It will be on July the twenty-seventh—three days after we break up," said the head-girl in tones almost as gloomy as Joey's.

"Well," said Evadne—and she pronounced it "Waal"— "Well, I suppose she must get married *some* time; but I wish she'd left it till *we* were through with school!"

This was the general feeling for the moment. No one could imagine the Chalet School without Miss Bettany.

"Who will be headmistress next term, then?" inquired Elisaveta.

"Mademoiselle will," said Joey. Then she got up from the grass. "I just want to say one thing. I think you're all jolly selfish about it! She wants to be married, and she has every right to be. It's just as rotten for everyone, 'cos Marie and Eigen will be going with her, and she's going to take Rufus too. So do stop grousing about it—when *we* are round, anyhow! —and think of her a little!"

With this she stalked off, leaving the others staring after her.

"That is quite right," said Juliet. "After all, if it's bad for us, it's worse for Jo, because she will have to be here in term time, and she's never been away from Madame in her life. It's time the middles were going upstairs now."

The middles rose and went in silence. They were thinking hard enough, though.

CHAPTER XIV

THE STRANGE MEN AGAIN

NATURALLY, after that piece of news, nothing else had any chance of occupying the thoughts of the school all the next week. The girls were divided between sorrow for themselves, sympathy for Jo and the Robin, and rejoicings over the Head's happiness. Nothing else was mentioned, and lessons were rather sent to the background. Then, on the following Wednesday, a letter came for Elisaveta which turned the thoughts of them all to her concerns. Dr Tracy had written to say that her father had had a bad fall from his horse, and was suffering from concussion and a broken leg. At the same time the King had written to Miss Bettany to tell her that the Crown Prince was very ill, and that under no circumstances was his little daughter to attempt to come to him. If things went well, he would be out of danger in a short time; if they went badly, she would not be in time to see her father alive. In any case, Cosimo was a danger to the child, who was as great a favourite with the people of Belsornia as he was hated, and it was very necessary that there should be no public demonstration in her favour, as was almost certain to occur if anything happened to the Crown Prince.

Madge took the poor child to her study and kept her there for the rest of the day, with only Joey and the Robin to see her. A wire was expected hourly, for the King's letter had said that whichever way things went, they must move quickly. The Crown Prince had been poorly for some days before this occurred, and his only chance lay in preserving his strength as far as possible.

"You will tell me as soon as the wire comes," Elisaveta pleaded, clinging to Madge.

"Yes, darling. As soon as ever I hear," replied Madge, holding her closely. "Try to be brave. Remember Dr Tracy is a wonderful doctor. God willing, I believe he will pull your father through."

"Yes," whispered Elisaveta. "He is good and kind; but oh, there *is* only daddy!"

Madge could only kiss her again, with murmured words of comfort. Then she had to go to her class and leave her alone. The Robin came in ten minutes later, and snuggled up to where she sat on the couch. "Tante Marguerite sent me," she murmured. "*Poor* Elisaveta! Never mind; God will look after your papa, just as He did mine when he was in that horrid Russia. I used to ask Him every night, and He did. He's always splendid!"

Elisaveta smiled through her tears, and put her arms round the baby. "You are a darling!" she said chokily. "I think you are the dearest baby I've ever known."

"Tante Marguerite says so too," said the Robin comfortably.

The Princess nodded as she dried her eyes with fierce scrubbing on her handkerchief.

"Let's go out to the lake," suggested the Robin, slipping down from her seat. "We may if we like. Shall we?"

Elisaveta got up. "Yes," she said. "The lake is always beautiful."

They wandered out and down to the lake path, where the visitors were strolling about. The Robin led the way to the boat-landing, past the great Kron Prinz Karl. One of the pretty lake steamers was just coming in, gleaming spotlessly in the bright July sunshine. She was heavily laden; for a number of visitors were in her, coming to one or other of the big hotels which had been built round the lake. The two children watched her with interest as she drew into the little landing-stage, where porters were waiting to carry the luggage to its destination. Many people were watching her too, and they cast interested glances at the two who were quite obviously from the school which had grown up farther along the shore. The two were so very pretty—the Robin, brown and rosy and dimpled; Elisaveta, slim and graceful, with long brown curls tied back, and deep brown eyes set in a flower-like face.

They, themselves, were far too interested in the *Scholastika* and her passengers to heed anyone on shore, and they had not been standing five minutes before the Robin suddenly gave a little ecstatic crow of delight. "It's Gisela, and Bernhilda, and Wanda!" she cried. "Look, Elisaveta! Oh, how nice! Tantè Marguerite *will* be pleased!"

Elisaveta looked and saw three girls, all about eighteen years old, and all smiling and waving to the baby, who was dancing about excitedly. Even the Princess could not feel anything but delighted; she had heard so much about these three. Gisela had been the first head-girl of the Chalet School; Bernhilda was the elder sister of her own friend, Frieda; and Wanda von Eschenau had passed into a sort of fairy legend among the younger girls. When anyone said anything about Marie von Eschenau's looks, some one was always certain to say, "Oh, but think of Wanda! *She's* much, much lovelier!"

Elisaveta had grown to think of this wonderful girl as being like the fairy princess of one of her adored fairy-tales, and, for a wonder, she was not disappointed. Wanda von Eschenau was exquisitely lovely, with golden hair, deep violet eyes, and a skin of roses and lilies.

The three saw the Robin, and waved excitedly to her. They made a rush as soon as they could get to shore, and, catching her up, simply devoured her with kisses.

"What are you doing, *Bübchen?*" demanded Bernhilda, when at length they set her down and came to earth.

"I am with Elisaveta," explained the Robin. "She is sad because her father is ill; so we are here to watch the boat, instead of lessons."

The girls had heard of the little Princess of Belsornia, and at once turned to her with sympathetic smiles. "It was in the *Neue Freie Presse* this morning," said Gisela. "I am so sorry."

"Come," said the Robin eagerly. "You must come now —at once, to the Chalet!"

"But first speak to papa," said Gisela, half-turning to a slight dark man who had been watching them with a quiet smile.

The Robin at once went up to him, her face held up for a kiss. She knew Herr Marani very well, for she and the Bettanys and Juliet Carrick had often stayed with him and his family in Innsbruck. He gave in to her at once, and then she pulled him over to Elisaveta. "This is Elisaveta," she said.

He took the little hand in his. "I have heard of you, my child. I feel for you in your sorrow."

Elisaveta clung to his hand eagerly. "It *will* be all right, won't it?" she said. "He has Dr Tracy, and I'm asking God all the while."

The Tyrolean nodded gravely. Like all his race he was very deeply religious, with a simplicity of faith which could understand the child's own belief that if only she asked God for help, it *must* be all right. "It is safe with Him," he said in his gentle voice. "God and Our Lady will help you, however it goes."

Then he turned to the others. "Shall we not go to the Chalet?" he said.

They agreed at once; and while the Robin trotted ahead with Bernhilda and Wanda, Gisela and Herr Marani came in the rear, Elisaveta still holding fast to his hand. Two men, who had been the last to leave the steamer before she steamed away to Geisalm, farther up the lake, looked after them curiously. "Who is that?" growled the taller of the two, a handsome, dark man, whose beauty was marred by many lines and a haughty air.

"I do not know, Highness," replied his companion obsequiously.

"Ridolfo has sent one of his own men to guard the brat?" said the other.

The shorter man, who was evidently afraid of his friend, shook his head. "Indeed, Highness, I cannot tell you," he said earnestly.

His Highness, Prince Cosimo, heir after the Crown Prince to the throne of Belsornia, scowled in reply. "It would just be like Carol to make a fuss, and get him to do it," he growled. "They think as much of the brat as if she were a boy, and could inherit."

Maurús Ternikai looked anxious, as well he might. His master was never easy to get on with, and if anything went wrong with their carefully laid plans, he knew who would have to suffer for it.

Luckily, Cosimo turned down his own fear. "I am wrong, Ternikai. Why should they fear from me? Did I not go from His Most Gracious Majesty of Belsornia, after listening to the most scathing remarks on my latest escapade, as he was pleased to call it, without a murmur? Surely he must think that I am well on the road to reformation. It was a piece of luck that you should hit on her in the Zillerthal. We might have travelled the whole Continent over before we lighted on her, had it not been for that. You served me well then, and I shall not forget."

Ternikai looked gratified, but he still watched his royal master cautiously.

Cosimo glanced at him impatiently. "Good heavens, man, can you not cease to look at me as though you feared I should kick you if it pleased me? Now, remember, after this, no more Royal Highnesses! I am merely Signor Carlo Belsarni, travelling for pleasure, and to see the world, as all good Belsornians should do. What is the proverb? "See the world, and then thank God you are a Belsornian.'" He laughed.

Ternikai was swift to fall in with his humour, and when they turned in at the Stefanie, where rooms had been booked for Signor Ternikai and friend, they were both in high good humour.

Meanwhile, Elisaveta, quite unwitting of her danger, walked to the Chalet, saying very little, but feeling the fatherly protection in the warm hand that clasped hers.

They were met by the Head, who had a great gladness in her eyes. Catching Elisaveta in her arms, she said with a sob in her voice, "All is well, darling! A wire has just come, and your father has recovered consciousness. He will get better from the concussion soon, and the broken leg is only a matter of time."

Elisaveta clung to her. "Is it true?" she gasped.

"Quite true, honey. Here's the telegram!" She put it into the child's hand, and then turned to welcome her guests. "I am so glad to see you. It is splendid to have my old girls back again! We shall be going in to *Mittagessen* in a few minutes now. There will be great excitement when the girls see you."

They went in, leaving Elisaveta still standing, reading and re-reading the precious wire which had brought back her happiness. She forgot all about *Mittagessen* until Joey came to fetch her; then she could do nothing but beam at them all while she hugged it to her.

"Poor kiddy!" said Miss Bettany, watching her from the staff table. "She was heart-broken over the letter a while ago. I think she hardly realises that it is all right now."

Then the talk turned to the school and they forgot Elisaveta for the time being.

When the meal was over, Miss Bettany announced that as *three* old girls had come at once she would excuse all lessons for the afternoon, and they would have a picnic in the pine-woods instead.

Jo said "Won't it be gorgeous—a picnic in the woods! And it *is* so hot to-day! I say, Elisaveta," she went on in an undertone, "I'm awfully glad your father is getting better! We all are, you know. I expect it's partly that as well, really."

"What is?" asked Elisaveta, bewildered.

"Why, the hol., of course! We'll get Margia and the others, and go *Blaubeeren*-hunting, shall we? Then Marie might make us some jam—if we get enough, that is!"

"And don't eat all you pick," added Juliet, who had caught the last part of this speech. "Are you going to take Rufus, Joey?"

"Rather! Rufus loves picnics," replied Joey, who was devoted to the big St Bernard dog whom she had rescued from a watery grave when he was a puppy of a few days old. They all rushed about after the meal was over, getting ready, and nearly driving Marie to distraction with their demands. At last they were all ready, and then they set off, Rufus leading the way with big bounds, while the girls streamed along behind, carrying baskets full of everything they could find. They would have to be back early, so that the visitors might catch the last boat, as they had only come for the day, so they were all determined to make the most of their time.

The spot they made for was a cool, shady opening among the trees, where they often took their meals on holidays. They all knew it by this time, and the middles rushed gaily on ahead, to set their baskets down and make all their arrangements quickly. Marie had put the coffee into flasks, as it was forbidden to light a fire among the trees. It had been a very dry summer, and everything was like tinder. Flasks were not so romantic as a gipsy fire, as Joey remarked, but they did save trouble. The girls found their camping-ground, planted the things ready, and then went off on their various amusements, leaving Miss Bettany to entertain Herr Marani and the juniors, while they scattered, some to gather sticks to take home to Marie, who always declared that no sticks heated her stoves so well as those brought from the woods in handfuls; others to wander among the trees; and the members of that done-with society, the S.S.M., to gather bilberries for the jam they all loved.

The Robin had attached herself to Joey and Elisaveta, who picked together, so she kept them from making any wild experiments, as they had to look after her. It was just as well. Joey's imagination was given to running wild when she was excited, and generally led her—and other people—into scrapes. As it was, the three clambered about the lower slopes of the mountain, picking as fast as they could, and blueing their fingers and mouths with the berries. Their wanderings led them away from the others, and presently they found themselves near a little path which led over the shoulder of the mountain to Seespitz. It was little used, as it was a wearisome way, and only the folk of the Tiern Valley troubled it as a rule. This afternoon it lay in the hot sunshine, solitary and warm, with tiny green beetles creeping over it, and shy woodland things running along it. Joey pointed to a felled log which lay nearby. "Let's go and sit down for a minute or two," she said. "I'm awfully hot."

"And the Robin looks tired," Elisaveta chimed in.

"I'm not tireder than you are!!" said the Robin indignantly. "I can walk ever so.— Can't I. Zoë?"

"You can," agreed Joey. "All the same, it wouldn't be a bad idea to rest a bit before we go back. Come on!"

They trotted over to it, and disposed themselves comfortably on it.

"We've got lots of berries," said Elisaveta, tilting her basket to look at its contents the better. "D'you think there'll be enough for jam, Joey?"

"Rather! Enough—if the others have got as many as us —to make jam for the whole winter," declared Joey. "Ouf! I'm hot!" She mopped her face with a handkerchief that looked as if it had been used for a pen-wiper, and then leaned back against a branch which had been left on the log. "Let's sing," she proposed.

"Well, sing something *I* know," pleaded Elisaveta.

"Righto!" Joey wriggled a little farther back, and then opened her mouth:

Das liebe kleine Bäumchen hier ist.

The others took it up at the end of the first line, singing gaily of the dear little tree which had grown up with the singer. They all sang well, but Jo's was a golden voice, round and clear, with something of the unearthly sweetness of a chorister's notes in it. It filled the lazy summer air, and reached the ears of two who had come there to discuss their plans. At the sound they started.

"Boys' voices," said the smaller of the two.

"Noisy brats!" remarked his companion. But as the clear notes welled up, even he listened. The song finished, and there was a pause. Then the voices began again. They sang "The Woodman"; then there was silence.

"Go an fetch them here, Ternikai," said the bigger man.

CHAPTER XV

M. TERNIKAI LEARNS SOMETHING

THE children had stopped singing. They could not decide on what to sing next. Elisaveta was all for "Hark, Hark, the Lark"; the Robin wanted to sing "The Red Sarafan," which her mother had sung to her often when she was a baby; Joey inclined to "Das Lindenbaum."

"I don't know either that or Robin's song," said Elisaveta decisively. "We ought to sing something we all know—and we all know 'The Lark.'"

"I'm sick of it!" grumbled Joey. "If you *won't* sing

either of the other two"—"I can't!" Elisaveta chipped in —"at least let's sing something we haven't been yelling away at for the last month!"

"*Do* sing 'The Red Sarafan!'" implored the Robin. "Me, I will teach him to you."

Elisaveta shook her head. "I don't want to learn it," she said. "It's a horrid *Russian* song!"

"It was mamma's song!" said the baby quickly.

"Well, anyway, I'm not going to learn Russian! It's a hateful language, and they are hateful people!" Elisaveta was hot and tired, and she felt cross.

"It's a very beautiful language." Joey contradicted her. "Some of the Russian folk-stories are the loveliest in the world. But we won't sing if you are going to be bad-tempered about it!"

They were all getting rather quarrelsome, and what might have happened it is not hard to guess; but at that moment Ternikai appeared round the bend in the path. Elisaveta got to her feet, unconsciously assuming her little princess air. "*Grüss Gott*, Signor Ternikai," she said as he came up, giving him the pretty old greeting of the Tyrol. "Why are you here?"

He would have taken her hand and kissed it, but she drew back. Something in her was turning her against this very respectful and courteous stranger, even though he had told her that her father had him sent.

He flushed as she backed, and bit his lips angrily. Then he remembered that anger would be fatal to the schemes he and his master had in view, so he forced back his annoyance, and answered her humbly, "I am still watching over you, madame. The Little Lady of Belsornia shall have no cause to complain of my faithfulness." He spoke in Belsornian, which Jo was beginning to understand, though the Robin didn't know a word.

Elisaveta bowed. "You are very good, signor, but I am quite safe here. My head-mistress is just down there in the trees, and all the others are near."

Ternikai thought that it was just as well that his master had not ordered him to carry her off now, if that were the case. Then he caught Joey's big eyes fastened full on his face, and turned away from her. There was something in that steady gaze which he distrusted.

"These are two of my friends," said Elisaveta, waving

87

her hand to them. "La Signorina Josephine Bettany and La Signorina Robin Humphries."

He bowed to them, wishing, as he did so, that he could tell Joey to remove her gaze. The Robin had got behind Elisaveta, and was peeping at him from this place of refuge.

The man transferred his attention to the Princess. "I have read the newspapers, madame. I trust that his Royal Highness the Crown Prince is likely to do well?"

"He is much better already," replied Elisaveta, forgetting her dislike of him for the moment. "Madame has had a telegram, and it says that it is only a matter of time before he is quite recovered again."

If Ternikai was upset by this news he did not show it. On the contrary, he smiled, as if it was the best thing he had heard for years, and said, "I am rejoiced to hear it, madame. It would, indeed, be a terrible thing if anything were to happen to him. He is needed by the country!"

Elisaveta was not sure what she ought to say. Joey answered for her. "We are all glad that his Royal Highness is getting better," she said in her perfect, fluent French, which she guessed he knew, since Elisaveta had told her that it was the court language, and that most of the people of Belsornia could speak it. The Belsornian tongue, made up, as it is, of words taken from Italian, Rumanian, and Greek, is difficult to most foreigners; and even Jo herself, who generally excelled at languages, had not found it at all easy, though she had persuaded Elisaveta to speak it to her every day, so that she might learn it. It was one of her ambitions to know as many languages as she could. French and German were as natural to her as her mother-tongue now; and she knew enough Italian to have been able to manage quite well if she were ever stranded in Italy. Russian she had coaxed the Robin's father to teach her one holiday, when they had been up at the Sonnalpe, where he acted as secretary to Dr Jem. She could understand it fairly well, and could speak, though slowly. Her written Russian was very poor, but Captain Humphries let her write to him once a week, and he always corrected her letters, and returned them to her, with explanations of her mistakes written at the side.

Jo had no idea as yet what a very good thing it was that she had been seized with the craze for learning it during the last summer holidays. That knowledge was to come later. Now she listened to Ternikai's courteous reply to her

French, and then turned to Elisaveta. "It is time we were going down to join the others," she said.

Elisaveta nodded. "I know it is." She turned to the Belsornian. "Thank you, signor. As you see, I do not need you this afternoon. Please take a vacation from your task of watching me."

She made a little gesture of dismissal, and he had no other course but to obey it. He swept off his hat, which he had been wearing in deference to the heat of the sun, and made the three a low bow. Then he turned smartly and marched off.

Joey gazed after him. "That man has been a soldier," she said. "Elisaveta, I don't like him at all. I wonder why your people chose *him?* There must be nicer men in Belsornia, surely."

"I don't think I like him myself," replied Elisaveta, looking the way he had gone, with a troubled expression on her face.

"He is a *horrid* man!" proclaimed the Robin suddenly. "He was making fun of us all the time, and he pretended he wasn't."

"That is it exactly," said Joey. "I couldn't think what it was, 'cos he was most awfully polite. But it was just what the Robin says. He—he was mocking himself at us."

Elisaveta sighed. "I expect he thinks it's a fearful nuisance to have to look after me, she said. "It *is* a pity I'm not a boy."

"*I* think it's perfectly idiotic of you people to have that stupid law," remarked Joey. "I'm sure you would make a far better king than that horrid Prince Cosimo!"

"P'r'aps he'll get killed, like those people in the Bible," suggested Robin.

"No such luck!" replied Elisaveta gloomily.

Then they were joined by some of the others, and she had just time to warn the Robin to say nothing about their encounter to anyone else before they came up.

Meanwhile Maurús Ternikai rejoined his master, who was sitting on a boulder, impatiently awaiting him. "Well!" he snarled, as his spy came in sight. "You've been long enough! What had the brat to say for herself?"

"They have had a telegram, Highness," replied Ternikai. "It seems that his Royal Highness the Crown Prince is better, and is likely to recover soon."

There was a silence. Prince Cosimo was digesting this

unwelcome piece of news. Nothing would have pleased him better than to hear that his cousin was dying. He was not anxious to kidnap Elisaveta. He detested all children; and, apart from that, he knew that the people of Belsornia would be up in arms if anything happened to her. If Prince Carol were to die, there would be no need to worry about the child. He was the next heir to the throne, and, in self-defence, the King would be obliged to have him at the court, and treat him as the future monarch of the realm.

At length the Prince lifted his eyes from the ground to his servant's face. "Is there a good chance of getting her?" he asked.

"Do you mean to-day, Highness?"

"No, blockhead! I mean at any time."

Ternikai considered. "I do not know definitely, Highness. I should think it might be quite possible. At least I have established it in her Highness's mind that I am her secret bodyguard. To get her away ought to be easy."

"That is as well. Once let her be safely in my hands, and I can make what terms I choose with my dear cousin and his father. You must manage it, Ternikai."

He bowed in silent agreement with his master's orders, and when the Prince got up to go he followed him in the same silence. They went back along the path to their hotel, passing the Chalet party on their way. Prince Cosimo looked at the merry group with a sneer. He wondered what would happen when the Princess was discovered to be missing.

In their private sitting-room at the hotel he ordered wine, and then sat down to discuss plans with Ternikai. It was long before they could hit on anything that would enable them to get away with the child and be in safe hiding with her before her loss was discovered.

For a long time they sat, Ternikai suggesting plans which the Prince turned over in his mind and rejected, always in the most unpleasant manner.

Ternikai set his brains to work once more. This time he succeeded in evolving a scheme which his royal master was graciously pleased to approve. They sat for long working out all the details, but at last it seemed that everything was perfectly planned.

"It will do," said the Prince. "It cannot go wrong, and I shall be able to make my own terms. You shall not lose, my dear fellow, by helping me. That I promise you. When

I have settled things to my satisfaction I will reward you.
All must go well with this, and we shall succeed admir-
ably."

Probably he would have been right, only there was one
factor which he had not taken into account. That was Joey
Bettany. As he barely knew of her existence, he was scarcely to blame for that. Still, if he had realised what she was
he might have reconsidered his plans again.

CHAPTER XVI

THE THUNDERSTORM

THE day after the picnic was one of flatness. Neither
Elisaveta nor Joey had thought of mentioning anything to Miss Bettany about Signor Maurús Ternikai.
Joey, knowing of her sister's intentions, had taken it for
granted that he had every right to be where he was; and
Elisaveta, well-schooled in the care that is taken of royalty,
even of royalty which has no chance of ascending a throne,
also accepted his presence as something quite normal. The
Robin was told that it was a private matter between the
Princess, her father, and "Tante Marguerite," and that she
must say nothing about it to anybody. She had the vaguest
ideas on the subject of royalty, and bracketed Elisaveta in
her own mind with the princesses of the fairy tales she
loved. So no one knew anything about the meeting, which
would have relieved the mind of Prince Cosimo, who was
rather afraid that the children would talk, and so force him
to alter his plans somewhat. As nothing might have been
more likely, he was in a state of irritable ill-temper, which
made Signor Ternikai wish him out of the way.

As for the school, it tried to settle down once more, and
pay some attention to its lessons. It was not conspicuously

successful, and the staff had some reason to be annoyed when the day was over.

"The work has been disgraceful!" said Miss Maynard. "Those wretched children don't deserve to have any treat! Just look at this!"

She held up Joey Bettany's algebra book, with every sum she had done that morning scored through with crosses. Simultaneous equations were Joey's bugbear, and her attempts at working out problems on them were remarkable for not even being sense.

"Ghastly!" agreed Miss Wilson. "But, after all, they're not a scrap worse than Margia's map of North America. She has put the Rockies, the Andes, the Blue Mountains, the Alleghanies, *and* Cotopaxi—standing by itself in the middle of Virginia! —all into it! Well, I *ask* you!"

Mademoiselle, who chanced to be in the staff-room, added to the tale of woe. "Evadne was doing translation this morning," she said plantively in her own language. "Never shall I make her to understand my beautiful tongue; but at least I might expect that she may translate, though with lack of freedom. What has she done? Of the sentence, '*Il va se laver, en se tournant à la table, où on a placé la cuvette*,' she makes, 'He goes to wash himself, turning into a table where the forks have been put!' It is too much! I will not permit it, I. She must forfeit her playtime!"

The rest of the staff giggled. Evadne's French was something of a legend among them. She hated the language, and rarely made any real effort to learn it. Jocy's craze for learning as many languages as she could filled her with amazement. However, Mademoiselle was grievously upset at this last effort, and the young lady found herself condemned to correct every mistake in the translation she was supposed to have prepared a week ago, and write it out three times.

In the school-room she gave vent to her disgust at this. "It's rotten luck!" she said. "What do I want with French? Reckon I can get round the world without *her* all-fired flummery! The Tower of Babel was a real mean thing to do!"

"If anyone hears you talking slang, you'll get into trouble," Joey stated, driving her pen viciously into the ink-well on Elisaveta's desk. "French isn't one-half so piggish as algebra, anyway!"

"They're all vile," groaned Margia.

"Oh, be quiet!" snapped her friend, who had intended to spend her free time in writing a story, and resented Miss Maynard's remarks on her mathematics. "Who could think of algebra with you nagging away all the time!"

The sheer injustice of this remark held Margia dumb for the moment, and Joey hunched her shoulders well over her book.

At this inauspicious moment Elisaveta appeared and demanded the use of her own desk to write a letter.

"Get another!" growled Jo, whose temper was not improved by the discovery she had just made that she had set the sum down all wrong and would have to begin it all over again.

"Cross-patch!" commented Margia amiably.

"Cross-patch yourself!" snarled Jo.

Simone added the finishing touches. "But you have ze leetle black dog on your shoulders, is it not, my Jo?" she inquired.

That was *too* much. Glaring at her, Joey voiced the idea that it was better to be a cross-patch than a cry-baby; and anyway, it was no business of *hers!*

Simone, who hated to be at odds with her beloved Jo, turned pink, and her lip quivered ominously. "I—I am not a crrry-b-baby!" she declared in a wobbly voice.

"Yes, you are!" Jo was in one of her worst moods and was ready to quarrel with her own shadow if nothing appeared. "You are always on the howl! You ought to be in a kindergarten!"

"Well, you are no better!" said Frieda Mensch, so suddenly that everybody jumped. It was seldom that Frieda interfered with anyone. She had earned for herself the reputation of being the peace-maker in the middle school.

" 'Tisn't *your* business, either!" said Jo.

"Yes, it is! You are being most unkind to Simone!" declared Frieda. "*You* make her cry, Joey, and then you tease her! You are very horrid, and not a bit like a Guide!"

Jo rose with some dignity, collected her possessions, and marched off. This was more than she could stand. The others looked rather scared. Joey rarely lost her temper. When she did the whole school knew about it.

"That's *your* fault!" said Margia. "Oh, Simone, dry up! You're a perpetual water-spout! It's your own fault this time if Joey was mad with you. You had no right to say what you did to her!"

Simone wailed loudly at this, so they marched her out of the room and into the garden, where she could weep without bringing some one in authority down on them. As it was, Juliet came on the scene just as Margia and Marie von Eschenau had deposited her on a seat with the injunction to "mop up."

Juliet was in no very sweet temper herself, and Simone always cried very easily. The head-girl surveyed her with a bleak expression, and proceeded to make short work of her. "Crying *again,* Simone?" she said. "You'll turn into a fountain some day if you're not careful. Really, you might be a baby in the kindergarten. In fact, most of them seem to have more sense of what is expected from a school-girl than you have. Dry your eyes and stop being so silly this instant."

"I am u-unh-h-appy!" sobbed Simone.

"Well, I can't help that. There's no need to be a baby about it, even if you are unhappy," Juliet told her bracingly.

Simone choked down her sobs and shook herself free from the other two, convinced that no girl had ever been so cruelly treated as she was. "I w-will g-go away," she choked; and went off in the direction of the pine-woods.

When she had gone Juliet settled the other two. "I won't have bullying," she said. "You are to leave that child alone —do you hear? And I am surprised at you both!" Then she turned on her heel and left them.

All things considered, it was as well when bed-time came and the middles were packed off. There was a thunderous silence in their dormitories which was not usual, and when Joey banged down the window to its fullest extent before she got into bed Elisaveta thudded into her nest as if she meant to go through the mattress. Bianca gave vent to a series of indescribable sniffs—she had quarrelled with Jo over a tennis-court that evening—before *she* settled down. Then there was a deep stillness.

It had been oppressively hot all that day, which probably helped to account for the attack of bad temper which had assailed them all, and it was hotter now. Joey, always sensitive to atmospheric changes, moved restlessly. She turned on her side and looked out of the window. There had been very little sunlight throughout the day, and now the sky

94

was overcast with clouds of a heavy coppery hue. It was very still, even the trees were silent. There was no mistaking it; an outsize in thunderstorms was coming.

Elisaveta felt it also, and forgot that she was annoyed with anyone. "Jo," she whispered. "Jo! Is it thunder?"

"Yes," said Joey curtly. She was still feeling cross, and was by no means inclined to make friends yet.

Elisaveta slipped out of bed and pulled aside the curtain that divided her cubicle from Jo's. "Can I come in here?" she asked in scared tones. "I—I am afraid of thunder."

"Come if you like," said Joey ungraciously. "You'll get into a row if you're caught—that's all."

Elisaveta came and sat down on her bed. "I don't mind a row," she replied. "I'd rather have one than stay there alone."

A voice from the other side of the dormitory spoke plaintively. "May I also come, Joey? I, too, dislike thunder."

"All right." Joey was gradually recovering herself, but she was not quite right yet.

Bianca came and squatted at the foot of the much-tried bed. "Isn't it horrible?" she shuddered. "It is going to be a bad storm."

A low growl sounded at that moment, and the three shivered involuntarily. They were all highly-strung children, and there was something almost ominous in that distant roll.

"It's a long way away," said Joey in hushed tones.

The sound of footsteps outside told them that Mademoiselle, Miss Durrant, and Miss Wilson were going over to their own quarters at Le Petit Chalet. There came another growl, nearer this time. The storm was travelling fast. Elisaveta stretched out her hand and grasped Joey's, and Jo pulled her closer.

"Shall we go into my cubicle?" asked Bianca in quavering tones.

"N-no," said Joey slowly. "It's just as safe here, really, and I'd rather stay where I can see what's going on.—What do you think, Elisaveta?"

Elisaveta agreed with her. In any case the thin cubicle curtains would be little protection from the horrors of the lightning.

There came the sound of steps running upstairs. The

seniors were going to bed. There was no likelihood of their being allowed to sit up for a mere thunderstorm.

"I hope the Robin's all right," said Joey suddenly. "She's scared when it thunders."

"I expect some one has gone to see that the little ones are all safe," replied Bianca. "Do you think the others are awake?"

"Most likely." Joey suddenly gave a wriggle. "I say, sorry, both of you!"

"So am I," said Elisaveta.

"I also," added Bianca. There was no need for anyone to specify *why* she was sorry; they all knew.

A much louder growl startled them at this moment. The storm was coming up from the north-east, so the lightning did not trouble them yet. The thunder drowned the sound to the door opening, and they all jumped when the curtains were drawn back and Miss Bettany stood before them.

The girls looked at her doubtfully. They were not sure as to how she would take this deliberate breaking of rules. She only smiled at them, however. "So you are all together? she said. "Well, it *is* better when we are having a really unpleasant storm progressing Company makes it seem not quite so bad. I just came in to see if you had——"

The rest of her speech was drowned in a crash bigger than any they had heard yet. It had barely died away into the stillness when there came a vivid flash of lightning and another crash. Even Miss Bettany shrank back before the glare. Elisaveta buried her head in the bed-clothes, and Bianca opened her mouth to scream, but no one heard if she did it or not. Peal after peal of thunder broke over them, and the lightning had become almost incessant. In between whiles they could hear cries from the other girls, some of whom had been aroused from sleep. The Head made signs to them, for not even by shouting could she make herself heard, and then left them for a while.

Bianca had hidden her eyes in her arms and was lying doubled up on the bed, while Joey sat with her arms round the Princess and stared out at the storm with wide black eyes in a white face.

From Le Petit Chalet the lights were twinkling, until some one came and drew the jalousies close. That woke Joey from her dread. She pushed Elisaveta gently to one side and slipped out of bed.

"Where are you going, Jo?" screamed Elisaveta.

"To switch on the light!" yelled Joey in response. She raced across the room and tried to put it on. Unfortunately, the electricity in the atmosphere had affected the lighting, and nothing came of her efforts. Another brilliant flash lit up the room for a second, and Joey made her way back to bed. After it was over there was a pitchy darkness and a sudden silence.

Elisaveta lifted her head. "Oh, is it over?" she gasped.

Joey shook her head, quite forgetting that no one could see her in the gloom. She was fairly sure that it was anything but over. The silence continued some seconds and was far more horrifying than the noise had been. The door opened once more, showing the Head, her face as white as Joey's. She came over to the bed. Just as she reached them there was a frightful red glare, a dull shrieking noise sounded, and then a ball of crimson light flashed past the window and there was a most awful crash, which quite outdid anything which had previously happened.

Instinctively Miss Bettany caught the frightened group of children in her arms. At the same moment there arose to the open window strong fumes of sulphur, and the grass in the middle of the playing-field took fire and flared up.

Joey, raising her head cautiously, saw it, and shrieked again. Madge loosened herself from the clutch of the three, and crying, "Get up and dress at once!" sped from the room. Full well she knew the danger to the wooden chalets if the fire were allowed to get any hold.

It seemed to the girls as if everyone in the place had suddenly appeared in their field. Practically every house in the valley was of wood, and the whole place was tinderdry, since there had been no rain for weeks. The men of Briesau knew what a ghastly conflagration would occur unless the fire were put out instantly.

Joey, scrambling into a weird selection of garments, and, urging the others to do the same, caught up the bedroom jug of water, and dashed out of the dormitory, half-clad, and without either shoes or stockings.

Elisaveta, muttering "Keep your head, whatever happens," went after, dragging Bianca, who was too frightened to help herself, and they got downstairs, to find most of the others already there. Juliet was in charge, and she rose to the occasion magnificently.

Marshalling the motley crew into something like order, she marched them all out down the path and on to the lake shores. Practically everyone who was not fighting the flames was there. Rufus, who had got loose from his shed, rushed up to Joey, his tail between his legs, and whimpering violently. Snow, or even water, he could have understood; but not this red horror. Joey laid her hand mechanically on his neck. "What shall I do with the water, Juliet?" she asked dully.

"Nothing," replied Juliet. "Oh! If only the rain would come!"

Several people round her were echoing her prayer. If only it would rain all danger from the fire would be over. But the rain did not come, and overhead the lightning cut its way across the heavy skies, while the thunder rolled incessantly. Joey could stand there doing nothing no longer. She slipped away to the back of the fence and skirted round till she had reached the other side of the Chalet. It was a wild scene on which she came.

In the field people were digging a trench all round the fire, while some of the men were trying to beat it out with spades, boughs dragged from the trees, and old sacks, which others were constantly wetting by flinging water from buckets, jugs, bowls, over them. Near the house Joey could see her sister helping to dig another trench, while many of the staff were beside her. At the far side of the fence she could see Mademoiselle, Miss Durrant, and Grizel Cochrane bringing the little ones to safety. That brought the memory of the Robin to her, and she set off to meet them and see if she was safe. She had barely taken three steps when there was a cry from Miss Maynard, "The rain! The rain!"

It was taken up on all sides, and then the rain came! It had been a phenomenal storm in many ways, but the rain outdid everything else. It came with huge hailstones, which cut and stung, and covered the ground with a white sheet of five inches in depth in as many minutes. The fire had no chance at all under that. Mademoiselle and her little procession turned tail and fled back to Le Petit Chalet. The people made for the hotels; and the girls tore back to the house. Everyone arrived bruised, and, in some cases, cut with that awful shower, which lasted for two hours and effectually put an end to all fear from fire. Every window in the valley was smashed; cattle out in the storm were bruised and battered; and the inhabitants rose the next morning to find the sun shining down on a land covered with slush, and drenched to such an extent that people who went out at all that day literally waded in *mud!* Never had there been such a storm within the memory of man.

Before midday all the glass in Innsbruck and the surrounding towns had been bought up, and an army of glaziers had invaded the Tiern Valley.

A high wind had followed the storm, and the lake was a mass of angry water, which tossed the steamers wildly to and fro. All the trees had been stripped of their leaves, the flowers had been battered to pieces, and in the woods the ground was strewn with down-fallen pines.

The Chalet girls mourned over the spoiling of their field. In the centre was a huge hole, fully ten feet deep; all round, the ground was scored and torn up by the trenches the people had begun to dig. As for the cricket-pitch, Grizel Cochrane, surveying it late in the evening, declared that she didn't think it would ever be right again.

Herr Braun, who had come round to see what the damage was, consoled her. "It will need only fresh rolling," he said. "Let us be thankful, *mein Fraülein,* that it is no worse! The aerolite might have struck the house. See, such a little way away it fell. *Der Liebe Gott* has been good to us."

CHAPTER XVII

SIGNOR TERNIKAI MEETS THE HEAD

AFTER the storm, lessons were allowed to languish for the rest of the week. The girls were all exhausted, mentally and physically, by what had occurred, so the Head was merciful and spared them much work. On the morning after it was all over no one got up much before ten o'clock, and by the time *Frühstück* and prayers were done it was close on half-past eleven. They had two short lessons, finishing at the usual time, and in the afternoon they all packed into the train and went down to Spärtz, where they wandered about the streets, then went into the public gardens, where the one fountain—the Tyrol has fountains in all its towns and cities, and they are generally kept playing all the time—occupied the attention of the people who had brought their sketch-books and cameras, and then went on to the little museum.

They had *Kaffee* with Herr Anserl, whom they met in the chief street, and who insisted that they should go. His housekeeper nearly had a fit when she saw him marching in with nearly fifty girls in his wake; but she was a resourceful person, and had experience of him, so she sent Martha, the little maid, flying out to the *Konditorei* to buy up all the cakes she could, and produced sweet bread and glorious coffee while the girls admired the old master's treasures, and chattered with him as eagerly as if he were not one of the most dreaded teachers in the school. He enjoyed it all, and ate a huge meal himself, beaming on his guests like an amiable old giant, and telling the most delightful tales about trolls and other fairy people to the juniors, who swarmed all over him and considered him the dearest old man they had ever met. They returned to the valley by the last train, and walked home from Seespitz, for the lake-waters were still so rough that Miss Bettany thought it wiser not to take the steamer.

The next day lessons were finished at eleven, and they all packed up and went off for the rest of the day to the Scholastika end of the lake.

It was late when they got back, but the next day was Saturday, and they were able to rest. Games were, of course, at an end, but as it was only a fortnight to the end of terms that did not matter so much. The girls picnicked all day, for they had *Frühstück* up in the pine-woods, and then climbed up to the Bärenbad Alpe, where they had sandwiches, coffee, and wild strawberries which they had gathered on the way, together with the whipped cream which the people at the little *Gasthaus* supply at a cost of about threepence a saucer.

After *Mittagessen* they roamed about on the *alpe*, and were agreeably surprised when Marie and Eigen appeared with baskets containing buttered rolls, *Kuchen*, sent by Frau Pfeifen, and milk.

Sunday was spent as usual, and on Monday they started the term-end exams.

"I feel awfully fresh," remarked Joey, as she took her seat in the big school-room. "It wasn't a bad week, after all. I think it's a good idea to have a holiday like that just before we are examinated. You can think so much more clearly after it."

"Is that a hint?" laughed Miss Durrant, who had come into the room in time to over-hear this. "Well, we shall see by your papers whether it really is so." Then she called for silence, and began giving out the question papers.

Miss Bettany, having nothing to do at first, strolled out to the lake, accompanied by Mademoiselle. School-life for her was nearly over, and she had already got things as nearly into order as she could. There was little said between the two mistresses at first as they walked slowly along in the direction of Seespitz. At length Mademoiselle spoke. "We shall miss you next term, *chérie*. It will not be the same at all when you are up on the Sonnalpe and we are here in the valley."

Madge looked sober. "I hate giving up the school," she said. "I sometimes wish Jem had built his sanatorium here. But the air is not nearly so good as it is up there, and he has to think of that. It's done Mr Denny a world of good, you know, and as soon as he comes down here he is ill again."

A quick footstep behind them broke across her speech, and then a tall man, dressed in Tyrolese costume, with the green *Jäger* coat and breeches, and little hat with cock's feathers at the back, was speaking to them. "Pardon, gracious ladies, but I have not the honour to address Fraülein Bettany?"

"Yes," replied Madge, looking startled.

He bowed, sweeping off his hat with the gesture he had employed to the little girls when he had met them on the mountain-side, only now he was careful not to permit any mockery to show in his manner. "I am Maurús Ternikai, officer in the army of his gracious Majesty King Ridolpho of Belsornia."

Madge's face cleared. "Ah! Then you are the bodyguard sent by the King to watch over the little Princess Elisaveta? I am glad you are here, *mein Herr*."

"I thank you, madame," he replied. "It is an honour to be chosen to guard our Little Lady, and to do a Belsornian's humble best to save her from the plottings of his Highness Prince Cosimo."

"Do you think, then, that she is in danger from the Prince?" asked Madge, looking troubled.

He shrugged his shoulders. "Ah, madame, who can say? Cosimo is a danger to her little Highness as long the Crown Prince is alive. It is for that reason that his Majesty has graciously sent me to assist you in your task of guarding her."

"I must introduce you to my colleague and successor, Mademoiselle La Pattre," said the young Head. "Will you come with me?"

They walked on, overtaking Mademoiselle, who had not paused when Ternikai had spoken, and he was presented to the French-woman. She looked at him shrewdly. "You say you are from his Majesty, monsieur. May we not see your credentials?"

He bowed again, and drawing from his pocket a parchment offered it to them.

"Here is the written order of the King, sealed with his own seal, and signed by himself."

They took it and opened it. It was an official affair, purporting to come from the King, introducing Signor Maurús Ternikai, lately Captain in the Royal Household Guards, as the bodyguard asked by la Signorina Bettany on behalf of her Royal Highness the Princess Elisaveta Margherita of Belsornia. It begged la signorina to have every confidence in Signor Ternikai, and was signed with his Majesty's characteristic signature, "Ridolpho R. B."

They read it, and then Mademoiselle rolled it up again and put it into the bag she was carrying. "I thank you, signor," she said.

"And her Highness?" he queried.

"Her Royal Highness is at present in the school-room, undergoing an examination in mathematics," replied Madge.

"Then she is safe. It may be that there will be need to take her into hiding for a day or so," he said. "If Prince Cosimo should learn where she is he would, I fear, make a determined effort to kidnap her. She would prove an admirable hostage to him, for with her in his hands he could make what terms he wished with his Majesty—and Cosimo is not good."

They looked at each other in silence. What Signor Ternikai meant by it they were not sure, but something very wrong was clear. Miss Bettany spoke at last. "We are very glad that you are here, that being the case," she said.

Ternikai smiled. Then he held out his hand in farewell. She placed hers in it, expecting a shake. To her dismay he raised it to his lips. Madge Bettany had not spent some years abroad without learning that it was an ordinary custom, but though she was used to it with some of the fathers of her pupils, she had never felt annoyed by it. Now, she would have given worlds to rub her hand where his lips had touched it. She couldn't *quite* do that, but she drew it sharply away. As for Mademoiselle, she gave him no chance of treating her thus, for she merely bowed to him very freezingly. He left them after that, going on to Seespitz, where Prince Cosimo was waiting to hear if he had been able to establish himself with the Head of the school; while they turned back towards the school.

The first thing Madge did when he had gone was to get out her handkerchief and scrub her hand fiercely.

"I, also, should feel like that," observed Mademoiselle as she watched her. "What do you think of our bodyguard, Marguerite?"

"I dislike him," said Madge shortly.

"*Vraiment!* And for me, I *distrust* him!"

"Elise! What do you mean?"

"He looks at one too boldly. It is well to meet the eyes of all, but not in that way. It is as one who bluffs, as Evadne would say."

Madge stopped short in the path and faced her with troubled eyes. "Elise, do you mean that you do not think he is sent by the King?"

Mademoiselle shook her head. "I do not question that, *ma chère*. But it is quite possible that he is not what the King thinks him. And yet, why should I say that?"

Madge took a step backwards in her dismay. "Mademoiselle! That would be simply awful! If anything should happen that Cosimo should find out where Elisaveta is it may be necessary to trust him with a great deal, and I must have some one I can trust thoroughly. I had better wire them at the court to-day."

"Indeed, you can do nothing of the kind," returned Mademoiselle promptly. "That would be to tell the whole continent where she is. No; you must write, and if they say it is well, then you must trust him. That is all."

"Well, it's a ghastly proposition, and I'm beginning to wish I'd never undertaken her. Oh, *what* a term this has

103

been! In fact, what a year it has been! Measles last term! Matron, a thunderbolt, and a fire this! And now, all this on top of it all! There's only one thing to be thankful for!"

"And what is that?" asked Mademoiselle.

"It's been the first term since we started that Jo hasn't managed to do something to herself! I suppose I'd better be thankful for small mercies and rejoice that she's got through safely without bringing my heart into my mouth over something!"

By this time they had reached the gate of the school, so they went in, and there were met by an awful tale of how Joey Bettany had upset her desk, turning the ink over a new gym tunic.

"And both inkwells were full!" wailed Miss Durrant, who had come to tell the Head what had occurred. "Geography is next, you know, and they want red ink for their maps. You never saw such a sight in you lives! She's blue where she isn't red, and her tunic is ruined!"

"But what on earth was she doing to do that?" demanded her sister.

"She *says* the desk wasn't set up right, she thinks." replied the mistress. "It seemed all right to me. Anyhow, she's changing at this present moment, and Marie has taken her tunic to the kitchen to see what she can do with it."

Madge turned to Mademoiselle with a resigned look. "Did I say Joey had got through the term all right?" she said. "I spoke too soon. I do wonder what she will contrive to do next?"

CHAPTER XVIII

ELISAVETA IN DANGER, AND JOEY AS A DETECTIVE

" JOEY!—Joey, wake up! I want you!"

Joey Bettany moved uneasily and grunted. Elisaveta, who was standing beside her, bent over her and shook her vigorously. "*Joey, wake up!* I want you!"

This was more successful. With a deep sigh Joey opened her eyes, and then sat up so suddenly that she nearly banged her head against Elisaveta's chin.

"Ow!" said that young lady involuntarily, as she started back.

"Sorry!" Jo rubbed her eyes vigorously, and was wide-awake at last. "What under the stars do you want?" she demanded, speaking in her normal tones.

Elisaveta hushed her at once. "Be quiet! You'll wake Bianca if you yell like that, and she mustn't know!"

"Well, but what's *up?*" asked Jo, lowering her tones. "Are you sick, or anything?"

"No! If I was, I shouldn't be standing here!" declared the Princess. "When I'm sick, I *am* sick!"

"Then why on earth have you wakened me at this time of night?" protested Jo, who had been in the thick of a most thrilling dream and resented having it spoilt.

Elisaveta bent forward. " 'Cos there's some one standing outside down there, and I *think* it's that Ternikai man."

"Coo!" What can he want now?" Jo's dream was forgotten, and she reached her hand out for her dressing-gown.

"Where are you going?" asked Elisaveta.

"To see if it's him, of course!" was the cheerful and ungrammatical reply.

"Supposing it isn't?"

"Then I shall ask why they are trespassing. People have no right in our field at two o-clock in the morning—or any other time, as far as that goes, unless they are asked."

Jo was into her dressing-gown by this time, and the two stole quietly to the wide-open window and looked out.

There was no one to be seen, and no sounds came up to them either. Joey turned a disgusted look on her companion. "You silly ass! There's not a soul there!"

"But there *was!*" declared Elisaveta.

"You've dreamt it!"

"I didn't! I've been awake for ages, and I *know* I heard voices. It sounded like Belsornian too."

"Talk sense! Who on earth's going to talk Belsornian at two in the morning under our window—unless that Ternikai person is mad and talks to himself!"

"You can say what you like," persisted Elisaveta. "There *was* some one there, and I'm going out on to the balcony to see if I can see who it was."

She climbed on to the window-sill as she spoke, and swung herself out on to the little balcony. Joey followed her as a matter of course, and the two peered into the grayness of the July morning. They could see no one at first; then a figure loomed up dark against the shadows, and Maurús Ternikai came slowly towards the house. Elisaveta seized Joey's arm in a bruising grip. "It *is* him! What can he want?"

"Ask him and see," returned Joey practically. "P'r'aps he's brought a message from your father."

Elisaveta hung over the balcony rail and whistled a low fluting note. Joey did not know, but it was the call Belsornian cowherds use when they want to call each other. It carries a long way, even whistled as softly as she did it, and the man below heard it at once and looked up. He saw the two little figures on the balcony at once, and came nearer. "It is I—Ternikai, Highness," he called in low tones.

"I see it is," replied the Princess. "What do you want?"

"A word with you, Highness. Can you come down?"

"Not now," declared Joey for the Princess. "The place is all locked up and we couldn't get out without some one hearing us."

He looked up with a slight scowl. He had recognised the child who had stared so at him, and he was not anxious to meet her again. However, it was imperative that he should speak to the Princess as soon as possible. He had been prospecting round trying to find out by guess which was her window, and Prince Cosimo was within earshot, so he must make the best of things. "If the balcony will bear my weight, Highness, I could climb up."

"I should think it's strong enough for that," decided her Highness. "You can try, anyway."

"It would be better if *we* came down," said Joey. "You could catch us as we fell, and then, if we could stand on your shoulders, we could climb back. I think we'd better do that."

"What I have to say is for her Royal Highness alone," said Ternikai firmly.

"Well, I needn't listen," replied Jo with equal firmness. "If you want to speak to Elisaveta you've got to put up with me coming too. I promised to keep an eye on her, and I'm going to!"

Ternikai swore under his breath. He was very anxious to get the Princess by herself, and he distrusted this black-eyed child with the firm little chin with all his heart. It struck him that she was too clever, and he would have given anything to have got her out of the way somehow. However, he saw that there was no help for it, so he gave in, and the two retired to get into something more suitable for the interview than pyjamas and dressing-gowns.

Prince Cosimo joined him when they had disappeared. "Aren't they coming?" he growled.

"Yes, Highness. They have gone to put some garments on," replied Ternikai.

Two minutes later the children reappeared on the balcony, clad in their school-frocks.

Elisaveta climbed over the rail first. Joey held her wrists, then there was a low "Ready," and she dropped to the ground, Ternikai catching her neatly. Joey clambered over as soon as she was safely on the ground, and he was obliged to catch her with the same care as he had shown to the Princess. He would dearly have liked to let her fall, but he didn't dare. When she was safe he held out his hands to them. "Come. We will go a little farther away," he said. "Some one might see us here!"

"We can walk by ourselves, thank you," said Joey, drawing away. "Oh, and be careful of the mounds! Herr Braun hasn't had time to get them rolled yet."

He let his hands fall, realising that they would infinitely prefer to manage by themselves, and they went a little way away from the house.

"Have you brought a message from my father?" demanded the Princess, as he stopped.

"Yes, Highness," he said; "a message, and another friend." He raised his voice. "Belsarni!"

Prince Cosimo came towards them. He was doing a daring thing, but it was necessary that Elisaveta should think him another of her bodyguards. She had not seen him since she was six, and she had known him as a clean-shaven young man then. Now he was much older and wore a beard, which he had grown for his present purpose. Ternikai presented him with much ceremony. "May I present Signor Carlo Belsarni to you, madame? He is to be trusted as you trust myself."

The Princess looked at him. The gray dawn was approaching, and she could see him fairly well. At once a dim memory teased her. Where had she seen this man before?

Joey answered that in part. "Why, it's the other man!" she said; "the one at the station when we were coming from the Zillerthal!"

Cosimo started and regarded Joey with a malignant air. It was useless to deny that he had been there, for remembrance had dawned in the Princess's face, and he was afraid lest she should probe further and remember who he was. "La signorina is very clever," he said to Joey, with what she called "a *beastly* sneerish expression." "I am flattered that she remembers me at all."

"It was the weird way you behaved that made me remember," Joey assured him with unflattering readiness. "You bobbed about behind luggage as if you were funky of the police or something."

At this point Ternikai thought it diplomatic to interfere. "We have very little time for arrangements. If you, signorina, will permit Signor Belsarni to walk a little way with you, I will give her Highness his gracious Majesty's message."

Joey shook her black head. "Oh no," she said; "I'll walk three steps away, and you can *whisper* it. I'm not going anywhere with anybody."

She walked the three steps, and was thus out of earshot of a low voice. Ternikai would have enjoyed wringing her neck at the moment, but the time was going and he had a good deal to say, so he was forced to agree. He bent down to Elisaveta and murmured, "Your Royal Highness would have been advised to come alone. There is much to say, and it is a secret."

"Then hurry up and say it," returned Elisaveta, standing very upright. "As for coming alone, a Princess of Belsornia always has her lady-in-waiting with her." This was true, and, anyway, too much time had already been wasted on things that really didn't matter. The cowherds would soon be coming along with their strings of patient cattle, leading them to the mountain pastures, and neither of the men wanted to be seen in the grounds of the Chalet School.

"I beg your pardon, madame," he said gravely. "I will tell you at once. There is danger for you here. Cosimo has discovered where you are, and it is the wish of his Majesty the King, and of his Royal Highness the Crown Prince, that you come away with me into a place of safety until the danger is passed."

"How do I know that you come from the King?" asked the Princess.

For reply he offered her a sealed envelope. "The instructions are here, madame," he said.

Elisaveta took it and broke the seal. Inside was a letter written on the King's private note-paper—Cosimo had a spy in the palace—and in the King's handwriting. It was very brief, and simply ran: "Elisaveta,—Obey the bearer of this in all things. He has my fullest confidence.—Ridolpho R."

It was in her grandfather's peculiar script—Cosimo was gifted in the art of forgery—and she saw no reason to doubt it. "Joey!" she called.

Joey was beside her and reading the note before either of the men could prevent it. "Coo!" she said when she had finished it. "What have you to do?"

"I am to go into hiding at once," replied the Princess.

"What? Now?"

Cosimo turned to his friend "Curse this brat!" he said in Russian. "Will she rouse the whole valley?"

With a great effort Joey controlled herself. She had felt that all was not well. This unguarded speech of the Prince's made her determined to keep with Elisaveta whatever happened.

Ternikai turned to the Princess. "Not this moment, madame," he said, "but soon. It is the request of his Majesty that you will speak of it to no one, lest Cosimo should make inquiries."

Prince Cosimo spoke again. "Take her at once," he said

109

in his fluent Russian. "Leave it now and something will happen. That child knows too much!"

Ternikai looked doubtful, but something in his master's face convinced him that it was the only thing to do. "Will it please you to come, Highness?" he said to the Princess. "Believe me, it is better so."

Elisaveta looked dismayed. "I cannot come now," she said. "I am not ready."

"You can get a hat and coat if I put you up," urged the man. "I will lift you and la signorina, and she can help you to come down again. It is best." Then he added the one thing that was needed to persuade her. "For the good of the kingdom, Highness. It is necessary."

Elisaveta turned to Joey. "I must," she said. "Come on!"

Joey turned and went across the grass with her without a word. She was too busy thinking to say anything. The story *might* be true. She had very little to go on, for she had only followed Cosimo's Russian very roughly, and she might have got it all wrong. Anyway, she would have to let Elisaveta go. *But*—and it was a big "but"—she would keep her promise and go too. Only, the men would not know it. They climbed up and got back into the dormitory without any trouble. Elisaveta collected her toothbrush, her comb, and some handkerchiefs. Joey helped her into her long coat and gave her her hat. Then she put her arms round her neck. "If anything goes wrong, or you are frightened, or anything," she said. "call three times like an owl. Don't let *them* know, though. Good-bye!"

She kissed her friend and then helped her through the window. Elisaveta dropped, and Cosimo caught her safely. Joey waved her hand and then went back into the room, rather to the surprise of the men, who had been sure that she would wait to see them off. Joey had other things to do, however, and she would have been ashamed of herself if she could not follow a track in the thick dews. She dressed herself warmly, took her purse, and also Elisaveta's, for she had no idea what she might want, and money was always a good thing to take with one on an expedition of this kind. Then she wrote a note to her sister, which she pinned to her pillow, and when they had had a good start she went out on to the balcony once more and let herself down on to the grass.

The Chalet School remained in stillness, although Bianca, vaguely disturbed. turned over in bed relentlessly.

However, she did not wake up, and by the time that Marie Pfeifen, always the first up, was stirring, the two members of the school were far enough away.

CHAPTER XIX

CONSTERNATION

THE rising bell had gone, and Bianca, drowsing comfortably among the sheets, was rather surprised that nobody made any effort to get her out of bed. As a rule it was only the exertions of Elisaveta and Joey that got her down to *Frühstück* in time, but to-day there was only silence from behind the curtains which hid the other beds from view. The window was wide open she knew, for her own curtains were drifting lazily backwards and forwards in the breeze. Finally she roused herself sufficiently to call, "Joey, what is the hour?"

There was no answer.

"Horrid things!" she thought. "They have got up and gone out early without waking me. Now I shall be late, and Maynie will be cross! Oh dear!"

As there seemed nothing else to do she rolled out of bed, snatched up her towels and made for the bathroom. It was so late that she only had what Joey called, "A cat's lick and a promise." Then she fled back to the bedroom and hurried through her dressing. With all her haste she wasn't nearly ready when the warning bell went, and even when she was dressed she had to turn all the clothes off her bed, carry them out, and hang them over the balcony rail to air. She grabbed them up, pushed the curtains aside, and then nearly dropped them. Joey's bed was just as she had got out of it! Well! Words failed Bianca. She scrambled through the window, hung up her burden anyhow, and made a dash for Jo's bed. The final bell sounded as she did so, but Bianca was a Guide, and she couldn't leave the bed like that. Jo would get into a most fearful row if

111

it were found. She stripped the bed at express speed and hauled the curtains back. Then she got her second bad shock. Elisaveta's bed was in the same condition! Well, there was nothing for it but to strip it too. Bianca did so, and then went down to *Speisesaal*, nearly ten minutes late.

As she came in Miss Bettany turned round. "Bianca, you are very late," she said severely. "And where are the other two?"

It was beyond Bianca. She stared dumbly at her head-mistress.

"Did you not hear my question?" demanded Miss Bettany with excusable annoyance. "I want to know why you three are all late for *Frühstück*—and where the other two are?"

Bianca found her voice. "I do not know, Madame," she said faintly. "I thought they would be here."

"You thought they would be here? Do you mean that you have not seen them this morning?"

"No, Madame."

"Then where are they?"

"I do not know, Madame."

Miss Bettany turned from Bianca to the rest. "Have any of you seen either of them?" Nobody had. Neither could anyone suggest where they could be. Bianca was sent to her seat, and the school was told to go on with its meal, while Miss Bettany returned to hers.

"Coo!" murmured Margia to her next-door neighbour, Frieda Mensch. "I wouldn't be those two for something! Where d'you suppose they are?"

Frieda had no ideas on the subject and conversation languished. As Grizel said afterwards, "How could anyone talk with Madame looking like a thunderstorm and an earthquake rolled into one?"

When grace had been said, Miss Bettany called the prefects to her study and told them to find other people to make their beds for them, and to go and look for the missing pair until the bell rang for prayers, or until they were found. Then she went to the Blue dormitory to see if she could find any clue to their absence there. She found Bianca making her own bed at the same express speed at which she had stripped. The curtains were thrown back in accordance with the rules, and the bedding of the two was all airing on the balcony.

With a sudden remembrance of the Italian child's lateness the Head turned to her. "Were those beds stripped when you got up, or did you do them?" she inquired.

Bianca stopped with her *plumeau* in her arms and shuffled uneasily from one foot to the other. She wasn't very sure what to say. She had no desire to get them into any further trouble and she couldn't tell a lie about it, so she said nothing, and brought wrath on her own devoted head.

"I am waiting for an answer, Bianca," the Head said, in such icy tones that the child gave it up.

"No, Madame, they weren't," she said unwillingly.

"Then who did it? You?"

"Y-yes, Madame."

"Is that why you were late?"

"No, not exactly," Bianca stammered.

"How do you mean! Were you late to start with?"

"Y-yes."

"I see. And, I suppose, you thought that as you *were* late a few minutes more could make no difference?"

Bianca's head went down, and her cheeks burned. She wondered if the Head was going to punish her very severely.

"It was mistaken kindness, Bianca," said Miss Bettany gravely. "You should not have done it. I will excuse your lateness this once, but you must be in time for the future."

Then she left the room, and Bianca, having finished her own work, set to work and made Elisaveta's bed. She turned to Joey's quarters next, and had got the under blanket and sheet nearly tucked in and was bringing the pillows, when she gave a little exclamation and dropped them. On one she had seen the note which Joey had left when she had gone off on her mad adventure. With hands trembling with eagerness Bianca unpinned it, and then tore down the stairs to the study, nearly knocking over Frieda as she went. Miss Bettany was there, talking to Miss Maynard, when she burst in without knocking. The Head looked up, annoyed. "Really, Bianca——" she began. Then she stopped as she saw the little note the girl held out, with its direction, "Madge," written in Joey's unmistakable scrawl.

"It was pinned to the pillow," panted Bianca, who was breathless with haste. "I did not see it when I stripped the bed."

The Head took it and tore it open. The two people in the study watched her face anxiously as she read it, and saw it change to a whiteness which made Miss Maynard step forward hastily and put an arm round her. "Go and fetch some water, Bianca," she said sharply. "Don't speak to anyone on the way."

Bianca vanished, looking thoroughly startled, and the mistress bent over her chief. "Don't try to talk yet," she said. "Wait a minute."

But Miss Bettany put her gently to one side and got to her feet. She swayed a little, but she pulled herself together and gave Miss Maynard the note. "Read it, will you?" she said. "I don't think I've taken it in quite."

Miss Maynard read the note rapidly. It was brief and to the point.

DEAR MADGE,—Elisaveta is in danger from Prince Cosimo, so the man who was sent here has taken her into hiding. I don't think he really was sent, as his friend talked Russian, and said we were brats, and other things. I promised you to keep an eye on her, so I've gone after them. Don't worry, and tell Jem, if he wants to follow us, I've left the trefoil every here and there. I've got some chalk in my pocket, and I'll draw it. Also, I've got my scout knife, and all the money E. and I have. *Don't worry!* And write or wire to Belsornia. The name of the friend is Carlo Belsarni. LOVE.—JOEY.

"Of all the mad things to do!" exclaimed Miss Maynard when she had got through this. Then she turned to the Head. "My dear, don't look like that! Joey's got her head screwed on the right way, and she hasn't been a Guide for nothing. Let me ring up Dr Jem, and send off that wire at once."

"Yes; at once," said Miss Bettany. "In the meantime get the school together—it's nearly time for prayers, isn't it?—and take prayers, and tell them that Elisaveta has gone to see some friends and taken Jo with her. Whatever happens, we must have as little talk as possible."

Miss Maynard agreed with her there. She went out; sent Marie off to the post with a telegram to Signor Calmori, the secretary of the Crown Prince, and rang up Dr Jem, who promised to come down at once. Then she rang the prayer-bell, and took prayers. After they were over she made the announcement, and sent the girls in to their exams., with Miss Wilson and Miss Carthew in charge. Miss Durrant was with the babies, and when she got back

114

to the study she found Mademoiselle with the Head. Bianca had been put on her honour not to mention anything until she was given leave.

Mademoiselle was standing in front of the window wringing her hands. "Never, never will I understand the girls of to-day!" she was crying. "When I was a child I should never have dreamed of going off like that, I—I should have told my elders, knowing that they would know if it were right for me to do so."

Miss Bettany raised her head with a faint smile. "I'm afraid it is partly my own fault, Elise. It is quite true I told Joey to look after Elisaveta. I never thought of her doing it to these lengths; but that is largely what has sent her, I feel sure. In any case we cannot do anything more till Dr Jem comes. Then I will set off at once to find the children, and I will never rest till I do."

"After all, it *may* be all right," put in Miss Maynard. "We've only what Joey imagines she heard this Carlo Belsarni say to go upon, and Jo's knowledge of Russian is not very full as yet."

Madge shook her head. "I don't know anything about Carlo Belsarni, but I do know that I have spoken to Signor Ternikai, and—I didn't like him."

"What are the girls to know?" asked Mademoiselle.

"Nothing—as yet. If it is all right, we should only be doing the very thing to bring Cosimo on their track; if it isn't, then I know that Belsornia won't want a fuss made to draw attention to it. I must wait until I hear from them."

How the morning passed after that not one of the three could quite say. Dr Jem appeared in about an hour's time, and he agreed that nothing could be done until word came from Belsornia. He sent Miss Maynard along to the Seespitz end of the lake to see if there were any trefoils drawn there, and went himself up the valley to see what he could find. The mistress returned first, to report a complete failure, but he came back saying that the symbol had been drawn on the fence between the valleys, and also on the farther side of the little footbridge which led over the dry bed of the river.

"They are going over the Tiern Pass, then," said Madge. "Well, we at least know that much!"

At fourteen o'clock—two, in English time—an answer arrived from Belsornia. It came in an aeroplane, and in the shape of Captain Trevillion, one of the Crown Prince's equerries. He had flown from Belsornia on the receipt of Miss Maynard's very guarded telegram, made a landing at Eben, a little way down the mountain, and come on to Briesau as fast as his legs would carry him. He reached the Chalet when the girls were busy with afternoon exams., and asked to be taken to Miss Bettany at once.

She came to meet him, her face as white as a sheet. "I am sorry to have to tell you, Madame," he said, "that Carlo Belsarni is one of the aliases of Prince Cosimo. I am afraid he has kidnapped the Princess."

Madge stood in perfect silence. Dr Jem put his arm round her to steady her, for she was swaying as she stood. The captain looked surprised at the Head's emotion. "Miss Bettany's little sister has gone after them," said Dr Jem. "She said that she would follow them and leave a sign wherever she could to help us to track the party."

The captain's face relaxed. "I am sorry Madame," he said. "I will go at once, if you will tell me the sign."

"I am coming with you," said Madge, speaking in a toneless voice. "I will go and get ready."

She left the room, and the doctor turned to the other man, an eager question on his lips. "If Cosimo finds out what Joey is doing, will he hurt her?"

Captain Trevillion was silent for a moment. Then he spoke. "If Cosimo is in a good mood he may do no more than take her prisoner," he said.

"And if not?"

"Then God pity them both," replied the captain gravely. "Cosimo has a warped brain. I do not know what he is capable of."

There was a stillness in the room, then the doctor spoke again. "Miss Bettany must not know that—yet," he said.

"I agree," replied the other man. "God send we reach them in time."

And it was with those few sentences ringing in his head that Jem Russell set off with his future wife and the captain to find the two children.

CHAPTER XX

JOEY ON THE TRAIL

WHEN Jo Bettany set off on her mad chase she had a very definite plan in her mind. If possible she meant to keep Cosimo and Ternikai from knowing where she was. So long as they kept to the mountain regions that was all right. The dew would help her to track them, and even when it dried she expected to be able to follow them. She had always been good at tracking, and had learned to be very observant. It was just as she dropped on to the grass below her balcony that she had an idea which made all the difference to the adventure. She would take Rufus! As Miss Maynard had said, she had her head screwed on the right way, and she argued that his nose would be of great assistance supposing she were stumped. Besides that, Rufus would be a valuable bodyguard if the men tried to hurt either Elisaveta or herself. She went round to the shed where he spent the night and let him out, first clutching him round the neck and whispering that he must be very quiet.

Rufus always understood what his little mistress required of him, so he walked demurely out of his shelter and made no effort to express his delight except by low whines. Joey slipped her handkerchief through his collar, and the pair set off. Naturally what she should have done was to rouse her sister and let her arrange for the following of Elisaveta. But the sensible course never appealed to the younger Miss Bettany. Also, she was not sure how much Madge was supposed to know. Ternikai had been most impressive on the need for secrecy, and if it *were* all right, then it would never do for two or three people to know of the plan. Jo's idea was to follow the fugitives till she knew where they were, and to find out if these two men had any right to carry off the Princess. If they had, well and good, she would come home at once. If not, then she would bring Elisaveta with her. Jo had rather vague ideas as to the responsibility of her sister in the matter, and she was resolved to save her any trouble that was possible.

The course the three had taken was easily seen, for the heavy dews showed their tracks quite plainly. They had gone straight across the field, through the back gate, and on to the head of the valley. That meant that they were going over the Tiern Pass, and Joey guessed that they would be obliged to travel fairly slowly once they reached the foot of the Tiernjoch, for the path was a rough one, and Elisaveta was no climber. She herself was a good mountaineer for her age. She had climbed the Tiernjoch by herself as far as the narrow ledge, where accidents sometimes occurred, and she had been right to the summit with Herr Mensch, Frieda's father. She had no fear, therefore, of not being able to catch them up, so long as they did not turn off to the high road and use a motor.

The dawn was filling the sky with rosy clouds by the time she reached the foot of the great Tiernjoch, which hung frowningly over the green valley. She had stopped once, to get a drink of milk and a roll at the little *Gasthaus* beyond Lauterbach, the tiny hamlet near the head of the valley. She had also bought two more rolls, and some *Blaubeeren Torte*, for she guessed it might be difficult to get anything later on in the day. More she did not dare do, for it would cause talk, and, besides, she had no means of knowing how far her money had to go.

From the *Gasthaus* to the opening of the pass was a matter of five kilometres, and by the time she had got to the rocky path, which is the beginning of it, Joey felt somewhat tired. A little mountain stream fell over a miniature waterfall into a tiny pool, a little way away from the side of the road. Jo made for it, and, lying down on her face, drank thirstily. Rufus followed her example, and presently the two rose and went on, feeling much better.

"Thank goodness," said Joey to the dog, "we aren't likely to suffer from thirst. There are streams everywhere round here."

They marched at the slow mountaineer's pace which Herr Mensch had taught her, and which she knew she could keep up for some time longer. They had gone a very little way along the pass when they got the first clue as to the track. Hanging from a little point of rock, and blow-

118

ing idly about in the breeze, was a square of white material. Joey raced up to it eagerly and snatched it from its perch. She recognised it at once for one of the handkerchiefs Elisaveta had taken with her.

"Sensible kid," said Jo approvingly. "Now I know for certain that they've gone this way."

She tucked the handkerchief into her pocket and went on light-heartedly. She was now in a region which she did not know at all. The rocks overhung the path, a thing for which she was thankful. It was long past noonday and the sun was hot. Joey argued that the two men would not dare to hurry the Princess too much. Cosimo would not want to have her ill on his hands—by this time Joey had firmly made up her mind that it *was* Cosimo who had taken the Princess!—and she was not strong. It was obvious, therefore, that they would rest. The only thing was that they would not dare to rest long on the pass, which was a highway into Germany, so she must carry on for as long as she could.

It was nearly three o'clock by the sun when she finally sat down to eat her rolls. She ate her food slowly, then lay down at full length for a few minutes, and fell asleep. She slept for an hour; then she awoke, feeling very stiff, and full of horror at the time she had lost. She got to her feet and stumbled on. Luckily they came to another mountain stream before very long, and Joey knelt down and bathed her face and hands thoroughly in the water. She felt better after that and a long drink, and just as she rose to her feet she came on another clue.

There was a little bush of wild barberry on the other side of the stream, and tied to one of its branches was Elisaveta's hair-ribbon. Joey tore off her shoes and stockings, and waded through the clear water. When she had reached the bush she found that the ribbon had been tied so as to bend some of the smaller twigs together, and pointing up the mountain. The Guide sign for "Road to be followed"! How thankful she felt that she had given up a whole Saturday afternoon once to teach the woodcraft signs to Elisaveta! If it had not been for that she might have lost the trail.

Rufus was sniffing at the ribbon. Joey held it out to him. "Follow!" she said. The dog at once turned to sniff the ground, and then began to go forward up the steep mountain slope. Joey followed, clutching his collar firmly. It was

119

a hard climb, and it struck her that Cosimo must have had a bad time of it getting the Princess up here.

Going up was bad enough, but coming down would be infinitely worse. She wondered how ever she should get Elisaveta safely to the road again. She had cut her signs as she had promised. She did not like to trust too much chalk. If the rain came it would soon wash away her marks, but cutting was likely to last as long as it would be wanted.

Up and up! Joey began to think she never *would* reach the top of this awful path. She had to pause once or twice to rest her weary back and legs, but always she went on after a few minutes. Then suddenly Rufus stopped. The scent was at fault. He circled round and round looking for it, but found nothing, and finally plumped down on his haunches and sat there, looking at his mistress with his tongue hanging out of his mouth. He had done his best, but he couldn't follow scent that wasn't there.

Some children would have given it up after that but not Joey Bettany. "They must have got fed-up and carried her," she mused. "I'll bet it was that Ternikai man that had to do the carrying. I don't suppose they did anything but go straight on. I'll try that, anyhow! Come on, Rufus, old thing! You shall have a nice drink as soon as we come to a stream."

Rufus got up reluctantly and followed his mistress as she struggled on up the path. It got steeper, and it was all Joey could do to go on. What was more, the sun was setting and the darkness would come very soon in this place, overshadowed as it was by mountain peaks all round. Joey put her best foot foremost. She had no desire to spend the night on a mountain-path, though she had no objection to sleeping on an *alpe*. Suddenly she came to what looked like a complete stoppage, for a huge boulder was in the way, and she did not see how she could climb over or round it. Now it was Rufus's turn. He suddenly put his nose to the ground, uttered a low bark, and turned to the right of the obstacle. He had got the scent again. Joey, following him, discovered that it was just possible for her to scramble up by tiny projections in the rock, and guessed that it had been necessary to put the Princess down while one of the men went up first, and they pulled her up between them. It would be the only way in which they would ever get her beyond it. She cut her trefoil deep in the side of the soft rock, and then followed a scramble beside which anything that had gone before was mere child's play. When finally she was safely at the other side she was too exhausted to do anything but lie flat on the path and pant for breath. Rufus, on the other hand, wanted to go on. With all the instincts of his magnificent breed he was ready to kill himself in the search. He had got the scent once more and he was burning to follow it. However, it was his duty to stay by his little mistress, so he lay down and made the most of this brief rest.

At length Joey got up and went on. She was nearly at the end of the climb, for she had only gone a few metres farther when she found that she was looking up at a grassy edge. That put new life into her and she made good time for the next ten minutes. Finally she found herself on a long, narrow *alpe*, which seemed to extend right round the mountain. The night had fallen by this time and she was in darkness. "I can't go on," she thought. "I simply *must* rest, or I shall be all in and of no use to anybody. I wonder where I had better go?"

Rufus showed her. Pulling at her dress to persuade her to get up, he made for the rock wall. She followed him, stumbling with weariness, and presently they found themselves right under it. The dog turned to the left and she went with him. For four hundred metres they went forward, then a little stream blocked the way. Joey dropped beside it. She was done. Not even the knowledge that Elisaveta was being tortured could have got her to her feet just then. She lay over a boulder, worn out to the verge of tears. Rufus let her lie. The scent had died again at the water's edge, and he knew no reason to go farther. He plunged breast-deep into it and drank thirstily.

For minutes together Jo lay where she had fallen. Finally she pulled herself up and followed the dog's example. The cold water refreshed her, and she remembered that she had another roll in her pocket, as well as the *Blaubeeren Torte*. She fished them out, and, dividing scrupulously with Rufus, ate every crumb. Then she looked round for some sort of shelter for the night.

The air on these *alpes* is very chilly at night, even in the heart of the summer, and the dews are heavy. Joey knew that it would be madness to stay where she was. She had a very healthy dislike of being ill, and, in any case, Madge would have had worry enough when she found them without having to nurse one of them through an illness.

121

She looked up to the sky with a very weather-wise air. It was a clear night and the stars were blazing in the sky. The moon had not risen; she was nearly in the last quarter and would not come out till much later. Still, the stars gave enough light for Joey, and the sky told her that it was likely to be a fine night. She turned and looked at the dark mass of the rock-wall consideringly. It was more than likely that there would be some little hollow or cleft in it, where she could lie. She was so sleepy that she didn't much mind where it was, so long as she could go to sleep.

She decided to cross the little stream and see what there was to be had on the other side. It was only narrow, though it was fairly deep, considering. She went back a few steps and took a run, clearing it easily. Then she went cautiously forward, keeping to the wall. She had barely taken three steps when she heard a sound that almost caused her heart to stop beating. It was the call of an owl, uttered three times in succession.

Jo stopped dead. Elisaveta was here. She had not expected it. Yet when she came to think of it, it was one of the best places in which she could have been. The huge boulder in the path would stop most people from trying to get any farther on, for they would think that it was impossible to go on. Quite likely there were caves in the limestone; and it was obvious that no cattle were herded here. If there had been she must have heard something of them, for in the Tyrol every cow wears a bell round its neck, and the tinkling sounds of the bells carry far, especially on such a still night as this was. If there were no cows on the *alpe* then there would be no human beings. Nobody, therefore, would be there to report the arrival of the three strangers. Finally, it was comparatively near the Tiern See. Joey felt as if she had walked at least a hundred miles that day, but she knew that she could not have done even a quarter of that distance. Therefore they were well within the circuit of the Tiern Alps. Anyone looking for the child would naturally expect her abductor to have taken her as far away as possible, and, if it were not for Joey's Guidecraft, she might have been where she was all the summer without anyone's suspecting where she had been put. Joey suddenly felt very pleased with herself.

She could not let the cry pass without giving Elisaveta the assurance that help was near at hand. She repeated the call once. Then she went on, feeling her way very carefully and pausing between each step to listen.

It was as well that she did so. She had just moved forward very cautiously when she heard the sound of voices. She let herself down on to the long grass, Rufus dropping behind her with the same noiseless movement. It was a pet trick of his which Jo had taught him for the sake of showing Grizel that, big as he was, he could move without a sound. Perhaps the wise dog also scented danger. At any rate he "froze" as Joey had done, and they were practically invisible in the deep shadow of the crag. Two figures appeared coming out of the wall, so it seemed, and Joey recognised them at once as being Ternikai and Cosimo. They spoke in Russian, and she listened with all her might.

The Prince seemed to be in a bad temper. "Bah!" he sneered to his friend. "It was but an owl! You ought to be a woman, Ternikai! You have such sensitive nerves!"

Ternikai did not answer. Perhaps he was too furious at his master's taunt.

The Prince went on presently, "I shall make stiff terms, I can tell you, after all the trouble we have had to get the brat up here. My arms still ache with hauling her up that last bit of the path!"

Ternikai, who, as Joey had surmised, had had the heaviest part of the carrying, still said nothing. The Prince took a look round at the sky and the *alpe*, and then turned to go back to the place whence he had come. Then he turned to the other. "She will sleep to-night," he said. "Also, I think she does not as yet suspect?"

"No, Highness," replied Ternikai.

"Good! Then there will be no need to keep guard to-night, so we will both rest. To-morrow, I go down to the pass, and will get into Germany, from where it will be an easy matter to conduct negotiations. I anticipate no difficulty there. Carol adores the child's footprints, and he will go to any lengths to get her back. Upon my word, I've a good mind to make him abdicate!"

He burst into an uproarious laugh at his own joke. Then he went off, and Ternikai, after a final look round, followed him. Joey waited until they were inside, then she gave the owl's call again, and after that she settled down to wait in a corner of the rock, where, with Rufus forming a barrier between her and the outer world, she was soon asleep.

CHAPTER XXI

THE ESCAPE

JO was so worn out that she slept soundly, in spite of
the knowledge that Cosimo and his jackal lay within a
few metres of her, and that the most difficult part was
still to come. She guessed that it had taken the two men all
their time to get Elisaveta to this place. However she was
going to get the child back was a problem that might have
puzzled wiser heads than hers but she snuggled down under
the rock-wall and slept as only a tired child can sleep.

Rufus, who had also borne the burden of the day, slum-
bered profoundly, and it was the early dawn when he woke.
Jo was still far away, and when the big dog moved and
stretched himself, she never stirred.

With the rising of the sun Prince Cosimo set out for the
pass and the little village of Miedern Riss on the Isar,
where he hoped to get a boatman to take him as far as
possible—to Toltz, where he intended to get the train to
Munich. From Munich, if things went badly, it would be
easy for him to go on to the Schwartz Wald, where his
foster-mother lived—one of the very few beings who loved
him. She, as he knew, would do anything for him, and he
was relying on her to help him in his disgraceful plans.

The dark shadows of the western slopes of the mountain
still held the *alpe* in their grip, and he passed the dog and
the child without even suspecting that they were there. Clad
in his well-worn *Jäger* costume, with his face half-hidden
in a heavy beard and his hair down to his shoulders, there
was little to connect him with the Prince Cosimo of Monte
Carlo, and Paris, and Vienna, who had earned for himself
the reputation of being one of the best-dressed young men
in Europe. He swung whistling over the crisp grass and set
off down the path, while Joey and Rufus slept the sleep of

the weary; while Ternikai yawned widely, and went back to his bundle of hay in the cave where they had sheltered the night before; and while Elisaveta tossed uneasily on the heap of rugs they had arranged for a bed for her, muttering continually in her sleep.

Rufus, being of a hardy breed, needed less slumber than anyone else, and before the dew was off the grass he had roused up, stretched himself, and then gone to the stream to get a drink of water. Joey was the next to waken. It seemed to her as if she were coming up from a deep silence; then she heard the faint tinklings of the cow-bells from the valley, far below, and sat up suddenly, bumping her head with considerable force against the low roof of the little hollow in which she had been curled up.

"Blow!" she remarked very definitely. Then she looked round. Rufus was standing beside her, wagging his tail, and looking very pleased with himself. Joey flung an arm round his neck. "Where have you been, you old scoundrel?" she asked, hugging him. He bestowed a wide and wet kiss on her face, and she drew back. "I love you, old thing, but I don't love your kisses. I wonder what we can catch for *Frühstück?* Shouldn't think there's much up here."

She got up cautiously, listening for any sound; but Signor Ternikai was tired. He knew that Elisaveta couldn't possibly get away from there unaided, and he saw no reason why he should not make up for lost time. Joey was stiff and sore after yesterday's strenuous work, but she plunged her head and face in the stream and soon felt better.

Food for herself was not so hard to find as she had feared, for she presently came to a small patch of wild strawberries, and as there were plenty of ripe ones she had a good feast. Rufus was another matter, however. He couldn't eat fruit, and she felt worried about him. Rufus settled the matter himself. He found a baby rock-rabbit, and it vanished down his throat in two mouthfuls before his horrified mistress could prevent it. "You old cannibal!" she said. "How *could* you? It was only a baby, too!"

Rufus wagged his tail apologetically. He looked ashamed of himself, though he really could not see why she was vexed with him. It was only a rabbit, and there were thousands of them, and he was hungry.

"Never mind, old boy! You had to eat something, hadn't you?" said Joey.

Then she got up from the ground where she had been sitting and went on to the south-east of the mountain, where the *alpe* ended in a bare mountain-slope strewn with boulders. Jo looked at it consideringly. "I wonder if we could get down there, instead of going by the path?" she said aloud. "If we could only get down to where the forest begins, we could soon get home. It would be a big lift, too. It would cut off all that part of the pass." Then her mind wandered to her sister. "I hope they found my signs all right," she said to Rufus.

However, she knew that she must not rely on this too much. She must be prepared to do something herself. The question was—what? She looked down the steep side of the mountain again. It would be difficult, she thought, but not impossible.

Finally she decided to get back to Elisaveta and see how she was to get her friend away from Cosimo and Ternikai. How she was to do *that*, Joey had not the least idea; she supposed she should think of something when the time came. She turned, and went back the way she had come. She had just reached the stream when she suddenly stopped. There was her friend, washing her face in the water. Neither Cosimo nor his underling was there. Joey suspected a trap. With a word to the dog, which he obeyed at once, she dropped to the ground and lay still. Elisaveta finished her ablutions and then stood up, tossing back the long curls from her face as she wiped her hands on a big handkerchief. No one came to her, so Joey decided to risk something. She lifted herself a very little, and uttered a low "Coo-oo!" Elisaveta heard, and promptly turned and stared so plainly in the direction it had come that if anyone *had* been with her he must have noticed it at once. No one was there, however, so it didn't matter, but Joey resolved to give her friend lessons in the art of concealment as soon as possible. Now she raised her hand and rapidly morsed "All's well!" Then she sank back. She had done what she could; it was up to Elisaveta to make the next move.

The Princess took a look round; then she leaped over the stream, and came running to Joey, who wriggled in serpentine fashion towards the rock. Elisaveta followed her, and presently they were both safely in the shadow.

"Will they miss you?" asked Jo.

Elisaveta shook her head. "Cosimo went away this morning, and Ternikai sleeps even now," she said.

"Can you climb?" asked Joey.

"A little. I am tired, but I don't mind that. Oh, Joey, help me to get away now, before they can do anything to daddy! I heard them talking last night. I couldn't hear all they said, but I heard enough to know that Cosimo has some horrid plan of making grandpapa and daddy give him what he wants, and saying they will hurt me if they don't. Let's go at once, Joey."

Joey looked at her doubtfully. Elisaveta looked very white and tired, and not fit for the scramble they would have if they went by the way she had chosen. Still, it might make difficulties if Cosimo got in his messages first, so she made up her mind to risk it. "All right," she said. "Come on!"

They set off, Rufus galloping on ahead. Joey had the good sense to insist on their keeping close to the wall, so they were not seen when a badly-scared Ternikai came rushing out to the edge of the little plateau and stared along to see if the Princess, whom he had just missed on awaking, were there. He did not see them, so he hurried back to the cave to get his boots and his coat, before hastening along to the full extent of the *alpe* to find her.

By the time he had emerged once more, the two children had gone over the edge, near the wild-strawberry bed, at a spot Jo had noticed on coming back. It was a very little easier than the way at the end of the *alpe*, for it had one or two naked tree-trunks springing out of the earth, and she reckoned they could help themselves with them.

It never dawned on the man to look over. He fully expected to find the child wandering about the *alpe*, and that she would try to escape he didn't dream for one minute. So he hurried past them at full speed, calling loudly to her, while they were scrambling and slipping down the bare rock slope, Elisaveta clinging to Jo, and Jo holding fast to Rufus's mane. The dog chose the easiest way, and although they were bumped and scratched and bruised, they were managing to get down in some fashion.

Ternikai, finding nothing when he arrived at the southeastern extremity of the *alpe*, was horrified. To do him justice, he was afraid that the Princess must have tried to get away by the path up which they had brought her the previous evening, and in that case she would certainly hurt herself—perhaps badly. He tore back to the head of it, calling "Highness! Princess! Answer me!"

By the time he had reached it the two children had gone half-way down the bare slope, and had reached the worst bit of their journey.

"How on earth are we to get down there?" demanded Elisaveta, eying it askance. "There's not an atom of foothold, Joey. It looks rather as if we should have to *roll!*"

"We won't do that if we can help it!" declared Joey. "I want a *little* skin left on me, thank you! Now, what shall we do?"

It certainly was a nasty place. The ground had broken off here, and there was a precipitous drop of some ten feet. If they had had a rope it would have been all right. But they hadn't one. However, no Guide was going to be done that way. "Take off your stockings," Joey ordered, sitting down and taking off her own. When she had the two pairs before her she produced her knife, and slit them up. Then she tied the pieces together with reef-knots, which have the advantage of pulling tighter the more strain you put on them. Still, that was not nearly long enough. They would land on a fairly steep slope, and they dared not risk a drop.

"Our frocks?" suggested Elisaveta.

Joey shook her head. "No; I don't think we'd better do that. People might have fits if we wandered to Briesau in only knickers."

This was so true that the Princess said no more, but cast about in her mind for some substitute. "What about our vests?" she said.

Joey brightened up at once. "Good scheme! What an idiot I was not to think of them myself."

They undressed, and removed their cellular vests, getting into their clothes again at top speed. The knife came into use again, and then they had a rope just long enough. It looked frail, but neither was very big, and both were thin, so they hoped for the best.

"I'll wind it round this stump to get a purchase on it," said Joey. "Then you go down first, and I'll follow. Rufus must scramble. Luckily he's used to that, so it won't matter so much."

Elisaveta obeyed without a word. They had done rope-climbing in their gym, so she was able to get down very well on the whole. She had to drop a couple of feet, but she managed to steady herself against a piece of rock that jutted out. Then she called to Joey. "It's all right, Joey! Come down!"

Jo proceeded to knot the improvised rope round the rock, then she took a deep breath and let herself down. It was a risky proceeding, for the rope was wearing thin, but there was nothing else for it. She had got halfway down when it suddenly gave, and she fell. Luckily Elisaveta kept her head. Clutching at her rock with one hand, she grabbed Joey's frock with the other, and managed to check her fall. Jo bumped her elbow badly, and scratched her face, but she got on to her feet and leant against Elisaveta for a moment. Up above, Rufus was whining unhappily. He wanted to get to his mistress, but he did not see how he was to do it. Joey, fully recovered, looked up at him. "Come along, old man," she called.

"Wouf-wouf!" bayed Rufus.

Then, like the girls, he decided to make the best of a bad job. There was a flurry, a scramble, and a young earthquake came sliding down on the top of them. They both screamed, and grabbed at his long hairy jacket. A minute more and they were all three standing on the narrow ledge, shaky but safe. After that it was a comparatively easy matter to clamber down the slope, still clinging together, until they came to one of the little wayside streams which bubble up out of the earth on all sides in the district. They stopped here, and all three drank.

They took off their shoes and bathed their feet, as well as their hands and faces. Then Joey stood up and took her bearings. "The sun is nearly overhead," she said, looking down at her shadow. "That means it's about noon. I think we had better go on till we get to the forest, and then rest a bit. We ought to find *Blaubeeren* there, so we could get something to eat. I don't know about you, but I could eat an *elephant*, I'm so hungry!"

"I don't think I'm as hungry as all that," replied Elisaveta. "I *am* so tired! Joey, do you think it will be long before we are back at the school?"

Joey shook her head. "Couldn't say. You see, I don't know how far along the pass we are. We must be a good way along, but I don't know how much. And we may have to go back when we are going through the wood. I don't know this part at all."

She looked at her friend anxiously as she said this. Elisaveta was very white, and it was plain, even to Joey's inexperienced eyes, that she couldn't stand a great deal more. Her severe illness in the early part of the year had sapped her strength, and she had not yet fully recovered. Also, she was less accustomed to stand on her own feet than Joey, and the experiences of the last two days had told on her.

Joey held out her hand to the Princess. "Come along, 'Veta," she said coaxingly. "We can't stay here. It's too open. There'll be shelter in the wood, and we can have a sleep. Rufus won't let anyone touch us, so it'll be quite all right."

Elisaveta remembered that she was a princess, and that princesses must keep up when it is necessary. Besides, the thought of what her father would suffer, if he got his cousin's demands before the wire Miss Bettany would be sure to send once they were safely back at school, helped to spur her on. Joey had her own reasons for wanting to get back as quickly as possible. For the first time since the adventure had begun she was beginning to doubt if she had done *quite* right in going off by herself as she had done. She only hoped that Madge had not worried too much, and it was a forlorn hope. As for Rufus, adventures were all very well, but he had had enough for one time. What *he* wanted was his comfortable shed, and the big plate of meat and bones his own servant, Marie, always prepared for him once a day. All three, therefore, were anxious to finish with this, and get back to safety once more. They went on very slowly, for the two little girls were footsore and weary, and at length came to the wood.

It was cool and pleasant under the trees; and the ground, carpeted with pine-needles, was soft to their feet after the hard way they had come. Joey led the way to a little clearing where the ground looked dry and warm, and they sank down beside the fallen trunk of a tree. Elisaveta fell asleep almost at once, with her head on Joey's lap, and Jo herself was not long in following her example. They slept for two hours. Then Rufus woke them by baying lustily. Joey woke in a fright. She thought that Cosimo or Ternikai must have got on their track, but it was only a bird that had flown rather near, disturbing the big dog.

The sun showed that it was long past *Kaffee,* and Jo decided that they must get home to-night. She shook Elisaveta awake, and they set out once more. It wasn't so far from where they had come to the head of the pass, and, though they did not know it, help was very near.

Joey left the guiding part of the business to Rufus, trusting to the dog's wisdom to get them on to the road. She did wisely in doing this.

Rufus led them straight to the edge of the forest, and they found themselves on the pass, just above the valley.

"Come on," said Joey with some return of briskness when she discovered this. "We shall soon be home now."

They made what haste they could, and then, just as they had reached a bend in the road, there came a sound that was sweeter than the sweetest music in Jo's ears. A man's voice said, "Don't worry, Madame. We will take you back, for you are worn out, and then Russell and I will come back and look till we find them. I promise it."

The dearest voice in all the world answered him. "You are very kind, Captain Trevillion, but I cannot go back till I know they are both safe."

"Madge!" Joey did not pause to consider how she had got there. Grabbing at Elisaveta she rushed forward. "Madge!" she cried. "Madge! We're here! We're safe!"

Some one caught the Princess from her grasp, and she tripped on a stone and fell forward into a very haven of safety—Madge's arms. She was held closely to her sister; kisses were literally showered on her face, and Madge's voice cried, "Safe at last! Oh, thank God! —thank God!"

CHAPTER XXII

THE RETURN TO SCHOOL

"JOEY-BABA!"

Joey, lying nestled in her sister's arms, looked up. "Madge! It's so nice to be with you again! I sometimes thought I never *should* get back! Once or twice when we were coming down the mountain and we slipped I thought it was going to be the wind-up!"

Madge held the child tightly to her. "We won't say anything about it, Joey. I don't want even to think of it!"

Jo's eyes darted swiftly to her sister's face. "It has been —bad?"

Jem Russell spoke authoritatively at once. "Jo! You are not to talk about it at all. Why can't you follow Elisaveta's example?" He glanced down at the little Princess who was lying sound asleep in his arms.

Joey shook her head. "I can't!"

"Well, don't talk, at any rate."

Joey lay quiet, but Madge, holding her, could feel her heart beating rapidly, and naturally felt very anxious about it. If Joey were to be ill, she didn't know what she would do. She felt that she could stand nothing more. It was a relief when they came to the road that led to the lake shore, for that meant that they would soon be home now.

It was growing late, and the dusk had fallen when they finally arrived at the gate of the school. Captain Trevillion wanted to take the child from Madge, but she refused. "She's wide-awake, and I think she would rather walk.— Wouldn't you, Jo?"

Joey nodded as she was put down. She felt dreadfully tired, and she was beginning to wonder if she would ever leave off aching, but she had enough go left in her to walk up the path and into the house. She looked round at the dear, familiar surroundings with a deep sigh. "How lovely it is!" she said involuntarily.

Madge smiled. "It's home, isn't it, Joey? Come along; you and Elisaveta must have something to eat, and then get off to bed at once."

"Rufus, too," said Joey. "He's been a *hero!* I could never have got Elisaveta away if it hadn't been for him!"

"Rufus shall have as much as ever he can eat," returned her sister, pulling one of his soft ears. "I shall love Rufus always for this."

Dr Jem had carried Elisaveta into the house by this time and laid her on the couch in the study. Now he came back for Joey. She refused to let him carry her, but he insisted on her going in at once. Marie was ready for them, with big bowls of soup, and when they had taken this they were packed off to bed.

The Princess—who had to be wakened before they could get her to take her soup—was to go into the sanatorium with Miss Maynard, to sleep with her; while Jo was to share her sister's room. The doctor thought it better that they should be separated for a day or two. He felt anxious about them, particularly Joey, who was highly excitable and easily ran a temperature.

Elisaveta was so tired that she fell asleep while they were undressing her, and never wakened when Miss Maynard sponged her down and dried her, and put her into clean pyjamas and tucked her up comfortably. Captain Trevillion waited until he was allowed to see her fast asleep in bed, then he went off to Eben, where his aeroplane and the mechanic who had come with him were waiting for him. It was a beautifully fine night, with blazing stars, and a bright moon to come up later on. He hoped to be in Firarto very shortly, and be able to relieve the anxiety of the King himself. In case anything delayed him, Madge was to wire to the Crown Prince's secretary in the morning a message which would tell no one outside anything. Above all, it was hoped that nobody but the people most concerned would ever get to know of this outrage of Prince Cosimo.

"Do you think they will leave the Princess here after all that has happened?" asked Miss Bettany.

"If you will consent to keep her," replied the captain, "I think nothing is more likely. She is terribly tired just now, of course, but it is easy to see that she has gained enormously under your care, and I do not think Cosimo is likely to make another attempt to kidnap her. If I know anything about Ridolpho," he added grimly, "I should say that he will have Cosimo quietly disposed of in one of the fortresses. He must be mad. As I told Dr Russell, there is a queer kink in his brain, and if he were anybody but a prince he would have been shut up long ago. You need have no further anxiety on that account."

"I am glad to know that," she said simply.

"His Majesty will doubtless send an envoy to see you, if his Royal Highness does not come as soon as he is able."

Madge laughed. "It sounds frightfully important, Captain Trevillion. Well, we will wait for that. In the meantime, I will take the greatest care of her."

He nodded and went off for his flight. Madge waited till he had vanished into the darkness, then she went upstairs to her own room, where Joey was lying in the little camp-bed. "Hullo," she murmured, as her sister came into the room.

"Go to sleep, Joey," said Miss Bettany severely. "You oughtn't to be awake now! Do you know what the time is?"

"Not an idea!" yawned Jo. "Hai-yah! I *am* so sleepy! Good-night!"

She turned on her side, closed her eyes, and fell asleep. Dr Jem, who was watching, heaved a sigh of relief and set down a glass of something he had been holding. "Thank goodness!" he said in low tones. "I was afraid she would have to have this to make her sleep. Natural sleep is the best thing in the world for her. Don't let anyone wake either of them to-morrow. They must have their sleep out, and I don't believe they will wake one penny the worse for all this."

Madge nodded. "What a mercy! I was dreading an illness for them both. Are you sure, Jem?"

"As certain as I can be of anything. They are both cool, and resting comfortably. Elisaveta never troubled me, in any case. She's worn-out physically, of course, and will probably be fractious and tiresome till she's got over that. But it's only a matter of a few days at the most. Jo, I *was* worried about. She's such an excitable piece of goods that there's never any calculating how things will go with her. I haven't forgotten the scare she gave us over measles last term!"

"Neither have I," said the young lady's sister.

It was unlikely that anyone who had had anything to do with it *would* forget. Jo had distinguished herself by running up a temperature of 105°, and staying there for two days, after which she had returned to normal almost at once, and had been convalescent long before Frieda, who had never been over 100°, was able to get up. They had had a terrible fright those two days, and it was held as a joke against the patient.

"Keep them both very quiet for the rest of the week," were Dr Jem's final words as he went off to the Kron Prinz Karl, where he was to spend the night. "I'll look in before I go up yonder in the morning; but I don't suppose they will need anything but rest and good food."

"Am I to keep them alone, then?" demanded Miss Bettany, following him downstairs.

"Oh, if they want a visitor, they could have the Robin, or Frieda Mensch, or some one who can be trusted to be quiet," replied the doctor. "Don't let that imp Grizel Cochrane loose, though; and you might keep Evadne, and Margia, and the other excitable people away. That's all. And, above all, don't let them think themselves heroines or criminals!

134

If you could manage to treat it as an ordinary everyday occurrence it would be the best of all."

"I'll do my best, but I'm only human!" retorted Madge. "It's been a ghastly time, and I can't forget all at once!"

"I know, dear," he replied gravely. "I wish I could help you more, but I don't think I ought to stay away from the Sonnalpe any longer, even though I have young Maynard there to help me. He's quite young, and it's a big responsibility for him."

He said "Good-bye" after that, and went off, leaving Madge to lock up and then go upstairs to her room, where Joey lay sleeping so profoundly that it seemed as if nothing would wake her. Miss Bettany made haste to follow her example, and got to bed as quickly as she could. She was so tired that she fell asleep as soon as her head touched the pillow, and she never moved until Marie came in with a glass of milk for her the next morning.

"There must be no bells rung, Marie," said her young mistress, as she sat up and took the glass Marie held out to her. "The Herr Doktor says that the young ladies are to sleep till they wake of themselves. And will you tell the other young ladies that they must be very quiet? I will get up now, and go to see how Fraülein Elisaveta is this morning."

Marie nodded her head and went off gaily to spread abroad the news that the two had returned. Of course everyone in the school knew that they had gone off in quite a wrong way, but the girls had promised to say nothing about it to outsiders, so Miss Bettany hoped that it need not get round.

There were great rejoicings at *Frühstück* that morning, but everyone was very careful to be as quiet as possible.

Joey and Elisaveta slept the clock round, and then woke up, feeling very stiff and sore, but with nothing else, so far as their bodies were concerned, to remind them of their experience. The Princess ate her breakfast and then fell asleep again. Nature was repairing the damages in her own way, and she would be none the worse once she had slept off her weariness.

Joey, more excitable, sat up and demanded a book. "I'm all right," she argued, "only I don't want to get up. I feel nearly as sore as I did when I sprained my ankle on the ice the winter before last. I *may* stay in bed for a while longer, mayn't I?"

"Well, for the present, I think it might be as well," agreed her sister, who knew better than to say that she *must*. That would have been the surest way to set Joey longing to get up.

She was provided with a book and another pillow, and then she was left to herself. When Madge came back an hour later it was to find her small sister buried in the adventures of *Little Women*, and quite happy.

"How is Elisaveta?" she asked as she laid the book aside and looked approvingly at the plate of *Kalbsbraten mit Kartoffeln* which the Head had brought her. "I say, we could have done very nicely with this yesterday, I can tell you! I've never been so hungry in my life before!"

"It served you right," said Madge with the doctor's last command in her mind. "You were very naughty girls to go off as you did, and I'm not sorry that you paid for it. I shan't punish you any further, but you needn't come to us for any sympathy, for you won't get any."

That was all she said about it, but it was quite enough. Jo had feared that there would be a big fuss; she had feared more that her sister would be very much upset over it all. But to have it treated like a childish escapade, and to be told that she was a very naughty girl, as if she had been the Robin, took all the gilding off the ginger-bread. Elisaveta was treated to the same remarks, with the addition that though she was a princess, it didn't mean that she could go off as she had done.

"You were trusted to my care," said Miss Bettany with unusual severity, "and if you had stayed to think for one moment, you would have *known* that anything which you were told to hide from me—at least, anything so serious as your being sent into hiding—must be told to me first. You didn't give your father and your grandfather much credit for being gentlemen when you believed all *that* rigmarole, Elisaveta. I am very disappointed in you!"

Elisaveta hadn't one word to say for herself. It was all so true. As for Dr Jem, he roared with laughter when he heard how it had been dealt with. "It was just exactly what they needed," he said when he was grave once more. "I imagine they feel horribly small, and will be glad to forget all about it as soon as possible!"

They stayed in bed for the rest of the week, for they were both bruised and sore with their climbing, and as the others had been warned to say nothing about it to either of them, it was soon relegated to the limbo of the school affairs. Madge hoped that it would never be resurrected again, but she was to be disappointed there, though that came later on.

CHAPTER XXIII

THE GARDEN PARTY

ONE of the most important questions in the Chalet School at the end of each term was always, "What shall we do for the end of term?" They had had a concert—several, in fact. They had given a nativity play. One term they had had an exhibition of work of all kinds, and another they had given a folk-festival, when they had danced folk-dances and sung folk-songs, to the great enjoyment of their audience; for they had not kept to one country alone, but had shown the tarantella, the Schuhplattler, Norwegian dances, and the old English Morris and country dances. In addition to this, they had sung folk-songs of all the countries that were represented in the school, and had finished up with some of the lovely old German Leider. It really seemed, as Miss Bettany said, that they had done everything they could do.

"I'm afraid we shall have to begin to repeat ourselves," she said to the school, who had been called into consultation. "*Can* any one think of anything different?"

There was silence, while every one racked her brains.

"Could we give a kind of water festival?" suggested Grizel.

"I'm afraid not. You see we haven't any private baths where you could show your diving and swimming, and if we gave it in the lake we should have a far larger audience than we wanted."

"Should we arrange a little masque?" asked Bette Rincini.

"It would be delightful if we could; but I'm afraid we

137

couldn't do one long enough to make people think it was worth while having come for that only. We might combine it with something else, though."

Then Elisaveta had an idea—this was before she and Joey had gone off. "Let's give a garden party," she had suggested. "We could do the masque then, and give some dancing too."

It was hailed as a grand idea, and the staff had put their heads together and written a charming little masque among them. It was to be called "The Court of Queen Summer," and would give everybody something to do. Marie von Eschenau, the prettiest girl in the school, was to be Queen Summer, coming to hold her court in the world, and the others were to be flowers, trees, butterflies, moths, birds, the summer winds, rain, sunshine, and mists. They had rehearsed it thoroughly, and hoped it would be fine enough to give it in the garden, and to have the garden party. All the last week, before the Friday which was to be the dress rehearsal, when the friends of the school who lived in the valley were to come to see it, people kept going to the barometer and tapping it anxiously to see if it were going up or down.

Friday was a glorious day, and the dress rehearsal went off fairly well, though there were several mistakes made, and Miss Durrant, who was stage-manager, was seen to be tearing her hair in the background. Luckily, Friday's audience was not critical, and they enjoyed the pretty play immensely.

The girls went to bed feeling quite pleased with themselves on the whole. Excitement began the next morning at the early hour of six, when Marie, who had a window cubicle, tumbled out of bed and hung over the balcony rail, anxiously inspecting the sky and the lake. "It looks as if the weather would be very fine," she reported at length. "The mountains are covered with mists, but the sky is clear and blue, and the lake is smooth like a piece of glass."

"Topping!" said Joey enthusiastically from her cubicle at the other end of the room.

Bette, who was the prefect in charge of the dormitory, sat up in bed and uttered an exclamation of horror. "Marie! Come back at once! You are wearing nothing but your pyjamas! You deserve to catch a bad cold, and *then* you'll make a pretty queen with a red nose!"

138

Marie came back to bed reluctantly, but Bette was a prefect who was always obeyed, and she did not dare to linger on the balcony.

Joey, whose exploits had relegated her to a cubicle in the Yellow dormitory, which was half-way down the room, and who bitterly regretted that she had ever gone off as she had done, heaved a tremendous sigh. *"May* I go and look out, Bette?" she pleaded.

"Yes, if you put on your dressing-gown and bedroom slippers," replied Bette cautiously; "and come through *my* cubicle, Joey."

Joey scrambled into the necessary garments, and pattered down the dormitory to Bette's cubicle and out on to the balcony. She sniffed the air loudly and with enjoyment. "It's going to be a gorgeous day," she proclaimed. "All right, Bette, I'm going back to bed now. When can we get up?"

"Not for an hour yet, I hope!" groaned lazy Evadne, who loved her bed in the mornings, and hated getting up any sooner than she absolutely had to do.

"You can get up after half-past six, if you want to," replied Bette. "Do stop making that awful noise, Evadne! I didn't say you *must* get up—only that you *might!* If you want to lie till seven, you may. No one is going to stop you."

"Praise the stars for that!" and Evadne snuggled down under the bed-clothes with a sigh of relief.

"Dormouse!" said Margia scornfully.

"Dormouse nothing!" retorted a muffled voice. "I'm a Christian person who sees no use in dashing round before you have to!"

"I don't think you'd better talk," said the prefect warningly. "You may disturb other people, you know."

"It sounds like it!" chuckled Margia, as a bump overhead announced the fact that some one in the dormitory above them was turning out. "Wonder who that was? They'll bring the ceiling down on top of us if they barge round like that!"

"Grizel, I should think," said Joey. It's about where her bed is."

At that moment a voice from the balcony above was heard proclaiming to the world at large that it was a glorious morning, and that "those lazy Yellows weren't up yet!"

"Grizel it is!" laughed Bette. Then she tumbled out and went on to the balcony and looked up. "Grizel! Grizel!"

Grizel hung over her rail in a perilous manner. "Hello! So you *are* awake? I thought you were all sound asleep and dreaming of cakes and pie——"

She stopped suddenly, as a pillow flew past her into the garden. "*Now* you've torn it!" she continued, as she turned round to her dormitory. "That landed in the middle of the marguerites! I should think they'll be like pancakes by the time we collect that pillow. What an ass you are, Gertrud!"

Gertrud Steinbrücke, one of the oldest members of the school, laughed. "Not they! They'll come up all right. But you might slip something on and go down and fetch it, Grizel!"

"I daresay! It was your fault it got there; if you want it, go and get it yourself!"

A curly head appeared through another window farther along, and the Head called, "Girls—girls! What a noise you are making! You'll rouse the whole valley! If you feel so energetic you had better get up at once!"

"Good morning, Madame," cried Bette. "I hope we haven't wakened you!"

The Head laughed. "Oh no! I was reading!"

"May we really get up?" queried Grizel eagerly.

"Yes, if you like. Ask Marie for some milk and rolls when you get down, and don't go out of the garden and the field."

Then she withdrew, and Grizel rushed round the other dormitories to tell the occupants that they could get up if they liked, bringing much recrimination on herself for disturbing people who had *not* wakened early.

In the Yellow dormitory Joey and Margia hurled themselves through to Evadne and hauled her out of bed, protesting and shrieking.

"You've got to get up! You've got to get up!" chanted Joey. "Grab her bed-clothes, Margia! Come on, Dormouse! You're up now—and a jolly good thing too! You'll be getting as fat as a pig if you spend so much time in bed!"

Shrieks of laughter greeted this, for Evadne was as thin as she could be, with arms and legs like sticks. No matter what they gave her, she never seemed to get any fatter. All the past winter she had been dosed with codliver oil, much to her disgust, and it had made no difference that anyone

140

could see. She was healthy enough; but, as Joey had somewhat vulgarly expressed it, she "didn't pay for feeding."
There was a noise such as would have brought Nemesis on
them in less than no time had it been an ordinary day.
Luckily for them a good deal of licence was allowed on
such a morning, and getting-up was anything but the proper
and demure affair it generally was. Jo, flying through the
domitory on her way to the bathroom, was soaked by a
sponge hurled by Evadne, who, since she *was* up, was
determined to pay out her tormentors. Marie got tangled
in her sheets when she carried them out to the balcony to
air, and fell headlong into Bette's arms, which, as the prefect was not expecting her, caused a general upset, and Miss
Bettany appeared at the door to inquire if they were mur-
dering each other.

When at length they were downstairs, the majority of
them raced across to Le Petit Chalet, waving the rolls
Marie Pfeifen had given them, and, standing in a group,
serenaded its inhabitants with a rendering of "Clementine"
sung in various keys.

It was nearly seven when all this took place, so Mademoiselle contented herself by calling them all *méchantes* before she began to laugh. The babies, of course, were delighted, and got dressed at a rate which sent them downstairs long before the usual time.

The rest of the morning until *Mittagessen*, at twelve
o'clock, was a whirl of noise and laughter. Marie Pfeifen
got through her work for the day as quickly as she could,
and several of the children helped her. The seniors were
busy putting little tables in various nooks and corners of
the garden ready for tea, and the juniors acted as messengers and did odd jobs for everyone.

At two o'clock they all assembled in the field, dressed in
white frocks ready to receive their guests. Miss Bettany
looked at them proudly. They looked such a bonny, healthy
set of girls. She had always insisted that they should be
like a big family, and she felt that her efforts had been
crowned with success when she saw them as they stood
there. Then the parents began to arrive, and for an hour
or more they were kept busy welcoming them, and showing
them the garden, the school, and everything that was of
interest, besides a good deal that was not.

At three the girls slipped off to get ready for the masque,
and the staff, with the exception of Miss Durrant and Mr

Denny, who had trained them in the songs, began to usher the visitors into their seats which had been placed down the path and on the grass behind the path. The play itself was to take place in the other part of the garden, with the background of the trellis-work covered with climbing roses, clematis, passion flower, and virginian creeper. When the last guest had been seated a little bell rang, and at once there rose the sound of the lovely old English round, "Summer is icumen in," sung by the whole school.

After it was over there was a moment's pause, and then a little figure in blue, with a taller one in the white and gold of the marguerite, danced in and spoke the return of summer to the earth. They were quickly followed by Heartsease, Narcissus, Lily, Dahlia, Grass, and Sunflower, while the Trees marched along, very tall and proud. A merry dance followed, "Up Tails All." Then the Flowers scattered, and Butterflies, Bees, and Moths fluttered in, singing *"Lieber Tag,"* a Tyrolean song. The Flowers joined in, and the harmony of the young voices was so sweet that people passing outside paused to listen.

Finally there was the sound of a horn, and then the South Wind, the Herald of Summer, strode in. Clad in a short blue tunic, with her black hair banded with a wreath of buds, and her hunter's horn wreathed in roses, Joey looked almost pretty for once in her life. She marched forward, blowing lustily, and then, standing in the midst of the pretty groups of Flowers and Insects, sang "Enter Summer," a dainty little composition of Mr Denny's, written expressly for the play. No time was allowed for applause, or she would have had an encore, for her voice was sweet and true as a bird's. Just as she finished there came a chiming of bells—cow-bells, borrowed for the occasion and rung by Marie, Eigen, Miss Durrant, and Mr Denny—and Queen Summer entered with her court.

Marie von Eschenau had never looked lovelier than at that moment when she passed slowly over the summer grass in her white gown with its edgings of summer flowers, her hand full of roses, and a wreath of marguerites, gentians, and alpen-roses on her golden hair. She was followed by her courtiers, the other Winds, the Birds, and the remainder of the Flowers. Strewing flowers in front of her were the two youngest children in the school, Inga Eriksen and Robin Humphries, dressed as alpen-roses, and looking delightfully important.

Queen Summer paused in the middle of her loyal subjects, and stood there, her hands outspread while she spoke a speech of welcome to all present.

It had taken six weeks and five people to get that speech into Marie, who was *not* clever, and who had had more than one weep over it, but everyone felt that it had been well worth all the trouble as they looked at her, and heard the words coming clear and musical from her. She was throned after that, and then the subjects of Summer came forward in turn, and, kneeling, offered her their gifts. The Flowers laid sheaves of their name-blossoms at her feet; the Trees presented branches of their leaves; the Butterflies, Moths, Birds, and Bees danced for her, and the whole court sang another song. Then Summer thanked them, and bade all join in a final merry round before Poppy should scatter her slumber-laden petals, and they danced "Sellenger's Round." The dance over, the courtiers fell into pretty groups, and, to the sound of "Golden Slumbers," sung by the South Wind, Poppy—Juliet—danced slowly in and out among the Flowers, who swayed backwards and forewards, slowly sinking, till they were all lying down in graceful attitudes. The Insects and Birds followed their example, and the masque ended with the grass covered with little masses of gay colours and living statuary, which Mr Denny declared were far more beautiful than any Greek ones he had ever seen.

A charming touch finished it, and this was an inspiration of the girls. While the audience was applauding lustily, Queen Summer rose from her throne, gathered up a great armful of her tributes, and went slowly over the grass to where the Head was sitting at the side between Frau Marani and Frau Mensch. The clapping died away as the people watched the child, wondering what she was going to do. Marie reached the chair. Then she knelt gracefully on one knee, and offered her lovely burden. "For Madame —with all our love," she said shyly.

Madge took the flowers slowly, her eyes pricking at the back. It was so unexpected and so delightful. She had known that these girls loved her—it would have been impossible for her not to know it—but for their affection to be shown as openly as this was totally unexpected.

The parents were almost as pleased as she was, and promptly applauded again, while she thanked her girls shyly. After that there was an interval for tea, during which the prefects acted as waitresses, while the younger girls went round making conversation.

At one of the tables sat a tall old man, with a magnificent head of white hair and a long beard to match. Miss Bettany paused beside him for a few minutes, and something he said brought the colour to her face. Then she turned and caught the Robin who was going past, and sent her for Joey.

That young lady left Frau von Eschenau reluctantly, and came to see what her sister wanted. The tall old man looked at her surprised. "But—is this the young lady?" he asked. "I had thought that it must be someone older."

"I'm nearly fifteen!" protested Jo.

He smiled. "Nearly fifteen, are you? Well, young lady, I suppose I do not seem a stranger to you? I know that my grand-daughter has my portrait in her cubicle, and she has told me that she shares a room with you."

Joey looked at him again. "Great stars!" she exclaimed. "You're the King!"

His Majesty, King Ridolpho of Belsornia, bowed to her. "You are right. Do you know why I want to speak to you?"

" 'Cos I'm Elisaveta's friend," replied Joey promptly.

"That is true; but there is more than that."

Jo went scarlet. "I—I suppose you think I ought to have looked after her better," she stammered.

He burst out laughing. "Not quite that! No, my child! I want to thank you for what you did in bringing her safely back. It would have been a terrible thing for Belsornia if anything had happened. Will you let me shake hands with you?"

Jo, with a knowledge of very stick fingers—she had been eating ices—looked rather dismayed, but she put them into his obediently, and then he stooped and kissed her affectionately on the cheek. "You will allow an old man the privilege," he said rather huskily.

To Jo's way of thinking she hadn't had much say in the matter; however, she promptly kissed him back, which pleased him immensely. Then he sent her to fetch Elisaveta to him, as she didn't know he was here.

"You are very good, sire," said Madge after the child had gone. "I blamed myself for not taking more care of her Highness."

"You took every care of her, Madame," he replied. "There was no blame attached to you. Even if there had been, the action of your little sister in going off as bravely as she did to fetch her back would have wiped it out of sight."

Then Elisaveta appeared, a rather dazed-looking Elisaveta, who was not accustomed to this amount of interest from her grandfather. She had, indeed, insisted that Joey must have made a mistake somehow, and had almost had to be dragged to the spot by that young lady. However, after that she never doubted again, for the King took her in his arms as if she had been the boy he had so longed for, and held her closely.

Later on, when Jo had been summoned to them again, she said, "Oh, your Majesty, what's happened to the Cosimo thing?"

"He is dead," said the King shortly.

"*Dead!* D'you mean you had him executed?" Joey was breathless with interest.

The King thought it best to tell them exactly what had happened. "He was found at the foot of a ravine not far from the German end of the pass," he said. "No one knows how it happened, but we think he must have slipped and fallen, breaking his neck. So there is nothing further to fear from him."

"I see," said Jo. She was silent for a minute or two, and his Majesty watched her with a smile. He wondered what she was thinking. It came.

"If he's dead, then who's the next heir?" demanded Jo.

The King's arm tightened round Elisaveta. "My little granddaughter," he said.

Two startled faces confronted him.

"Me!" gasped the Princess.

"Her!" exclaimed Joey. "But I thought you had the Salic law in Belsornia?"

The King nodded. "We had," he said. "Now it is done with, by the wish of the Grand Council and the two Houses of the State."

Joey thought a minute. "Will you take her away then?" she asked.

"No," said his Majesty, with decision. "She will stay here for another year. After that she must come home and learn the lessons that a future queen has to learn, even though she may never come to the throne. But then, I hope, she will not be alone."

He sent them off after that, for he had a good deal to say

to Madge, and some arrangements to make with her, and they only saw him to say "Good-bye."

Joey's opinion of him was delivered to the dormitory at large as they were going to bed that night. "He's a dear." she said. Then, as an afterthought, "It's a pity he's got such a scratchy beard, though!"

CHAPTER XXIV

THE WEDDING

JOEY was wakened quite early by someone pushing her, and crying, "Zoë—Zoë! Wake up, Zoë! It is Tante Marguerite's day! Wake up!"

Jo sat up in bed, her hair all on end, and looked at the Robin in startled fashion. "Goodness, Robin! Whatever time is it?"

The Robin shook her head. "I don't know," she said. "Come, Zoë! Tante Marguerite said last night that we could go to her first thing this morning!"

Jo burrowed under her pillow and produced her watch. "Five o'clock! She'd have something to say if we raked her out as early as this!"

The Robin's face fell. "How long must we wait?" she asked plaintively. "Tante Marguerite *did* say as soon as we woke up!"

"I daresay! But she never reckoned on our rooting her out at five o'clock in the morning," returned Joey. "It would be awfully mean to wake her now, Robin. She'd be as tired as tired at the end of the day if we did. Get into bed beside me, and we'll wait till half-past six. I honestly don't think we ought to go to her before."

The Robin gave a little sigh; but she was a reasonable small person, and she said no more, but climbed in beside Joey and snuggled down. "Isn't it quiet?" she asked presently.

"It always is after the term," replied Jo.

"So it is." There was a little silence, then the baby spoke again—very drowsily this time—"Zoë, will you tell me a story?"

Joey wriggled round into a more comfortable position and began at once. She was able to oblige with stories at any time, and this was one reason why the Robin thought her the most delightful playfellow there ever was. The story was all about a wicked old witch who stole little children and turned them into singing-birds. Then she shut them up in cages and made them sing for her whenever she wanted. Jo had got so far when she was interrupted.

"Supposing they couldn't sing?"

"They could—when she had finished with them," replied Jo darkly.

"I suppose it would be her magic." The Robin was very sleepy now. "Go on."

Joey went on, weaving a wonderful story about a little girl who *wouldn't* be turned into a singing-bird, so the witch said, "Very well! Then you shall be a pig!" and proceeded to carry out her words. She had got that far when she discovered that the Robin was fast asleep; and as she had no idea of wasting a perfectly good story on the air, she stopped, and turned her thoughts to the coming events. School had broken up on the Monday after the garden party, and many of the girls had gone away from the Tiern See until next term. The Mensches, the Maranis, the Rincinis, and the Steinbrückes, however, had all taken chalets for the summer holidays at various points round the lake, so there were still a good number of them left to come to the Head's wedding. It was to take place in the big school-room, which they had decorated the day before, and the English chaplain from Innsbruck was at the Kron Prinz Karl in readiness, for it was to take place early, as the honeymoon was to be spent in Italy, and they didn't want to break the journey.

When it was all over, and Madge and Dr Jem had gone away, Joey, Juliet, and the Robin were to go to the Maranis for a week, and then to the Mensches for another week. After that Madge and the doctor would return, and they were all going to Belsornia. The newly-married pair would be there only a few days, as Dr Jem did not think he could be spared from the Sonnalpe any longer; and while Joey and the Robin spent the rest of the holidays with Elisaveta, Captain Humphries and Miss Denny, sister of the school singing-master, would take Juliet to London and see her safely settled down at the university. Captain Humphries had some business to attend to in Devonshire, and Miss Denny would put in a round of visits, so it all fitted in very well.

Joey was sorry to lose Juliet, who had been like another sister to her during the two years she had been at the school, and it would be a year before they would meet again, as the elder girl was to stay in England until the long vacation. But just now her thoughts were with her sister. From the time she had been brought to England, a delicate baby of a few months old, she had never been away from Madge for any length of time. Of course she liked Jem very much, and he would be a topping brother; but all the same Joey felt sad, somehow, to think that she would no longer be the first in her sister's life. She would be at the chalet in term-time, and only go to the Sonnalpe for holidays. She wouldn't see Madge every day, and it would be *different!* Joey had a very conservative nature, and she hated changes. Of course she would still have the Robin! That was one comfort, but it *wouldn't* be the same!

Here Joey tossed so violently that she nearly landed on to the floor, which startled her and brought her to herself. The Robin was still sleeping, and it had only just chimed six, so she would have to stay where she was for a while yet. Then she decided that she needn't stay in bed, anyway, so she got up, dressed, and went out on to the balcony.

It was going to be another glorious day, for though the mountains were swathed in mist the sun was shining brightly, and the Tiern See lay like a sheet of glass, so blue that no words can describe its blueness. Joey leant against the balcony rail, gazing at it and thinking hard, when she felt a light touch on her shoulder, and turning, saw her sister all ready dressed for *Frühstück*.

"Hush!" whispered Miss Bettany. "Don't wake the Robin. Come along with me and we'll go for a short walk. I couldn't sleep either, so I thought I'd come and see if you were awake."

Joey slipped into the room like a ghost, and followed her sister downstairs and out into the fresh summer air, feeling happier. When they were clear of the garden and walking round the lake, Madge slipped her arm through the younger girl's. "Joey, you aren't happy," she said accusingly.

148

"Yes, I am," contradicted Jo. "It's only that I hate losing you!"

"You aren't losing me," said Madge quickly. "Do you really think I'd let you?"

Joey turned her head away, blinking back the tears that *would* come, and said with suspicious gruffness, "It isn't exactly *losing,* I know, but it won't ever be the same again. And if it wasn't that I like Jem so much, I'd hate him!" she wound up with a sudden burst of candour.

Madge pressed the arm she was holding. "I'm sorry, Joey. I can see your point of view, of course."

"I don't want you not to be married," Jo went on. "I'm jolly lucky to have had you so long! Only—well, anyway, I hope Jem knows how frightfully lucky he is! That's all!"

She glared ferociously at her sister, who promptly began to laugh. "Joey! Don't look like that! You look ready to eat poor Jem!"

Joey's face relaxed, and she joined in her sister's laughter. "It sounds mean and selfish, I know," she acknowledged, "but it's how I feel. Only, Madge, I do hope you'll be awfully happy, and have everything you want. Jem is a dear! ! I like him awfully. But you're the only sister I have."

Madge stooped and kissed the delicate face beside her. "Joey, it shall be just the same! *You're my* only sister, and I couldn't ever do without you!"

Jo brightened up once more, and flung her arms round her sister in an overpowering hug. "You're a sport! There never was a sister like you!"

"Thank you, Joey-Baba. I can say the same. Now I suppose we had better be going back, or the Robin will be waking up and looking for us."

They turned back to the house, and were met at the top of the stairs by a very reproachful young person. "You got up and left me alone, Zoë!" she said.

"I fetched her," said Madge. "Aren't you going to kiss me, baby?"

The Robin bestowed a hug and a kiss on her, and then consented to trot off and dress herself. When she was ready Joey led her along to Madge's room, and they had a nice little talk until *Frühstück,* which was at a quarter to eight. The rest of the morning seemed to go very quickly after that, and half-past nine saw Juliet, Joey, and the Robin dressed ready in their white bridesmaid's frocks, with big bouquets of red roses and carnations which Jem had brought from Innsbruck the previous evening, while the schoolroom was filled with guests who had come to see the marriage.

The civil wedding had taken place the day before, but there hadn't been any guests there—only the three girls and Dr Maynard, Miss Maynard's brother, who had come to join Dr Jem at the sanatorium. Now everyone who could manage it was there. Suddenly there was a little stir, and the door opened and Madge came up the room leaning on Herr Mensch's arm. She looked very lovely, Joey thought, in her shimmery white dress and soft veil, carrying red roses, like her bridesmaids. Then the child was aware that the chaplain was speaking and the service had begun. It was over very quickly, and Margaret Daphne Bettany had become Margaret Daphne Russell almost before she had realised it. The register was signed, and then they all went out into the garden, where Marie and Eigen were waiting with a splendid meal ready prepared.

It was a very jolly wedding. There were the speeches and toasts, without which no Tyroleans can ever manage such an affair, and Madge blushed scarlet when Herr Marani alluded to her as "Frau Doktor Russell."

They had forgotten all about trains in their enjoyment, so Madge had to be scuffled into her going away clothes.

At length she was ready, and it was time, for Jem was calling up the stairs to know if she would be much longer. "The padre has lent us his car," he said as she appeared, "so come along you people!" They were all packed in, and then set off along the side of the lake. As the car was a two-seater, and there were five of them, it was rather a squash. Madge took the Robin on her knee; Joey squeezed in beside them, and Juliet stood on the foot-board, holding on to the side, while Jem drove. The chaplain was to walk along after them, and he would drive the children back.

"It's very good of you," said Madge, as she gave him her hand. "Good-bye; and thank you very much."

"Good-bye, Mrs Russell," he said with a smile. "Good hunting!"

The visitors had gathered round them. There was a chorus of good wishes as the car began to move. Then Herr Marani set the example, throwing a handful of flowers at them, and everybody threw flowers after that, so that they left the Briesau peninsula looking, as Madge said, as if they were bound for Covent Garden.

Joey got a caterpillar down her neck, and nearly drove her sister wild by her frantic wriggles. "It's all very well," she complained, when Madge implored her to sit still. "The beastly thing's going farther down. I shall have to undress to get at it!"

Luckily they reached Seespitz just then, so Juliet kindly fished it out for her, and then they all ran for the train. The porter met them with a wide grin. He was another member of the Pfeifen family, and he knew all about what had been happening, of course. He helped them in, and tucked a bunch of alpen-roses into Madge's hand as he passed her case in. She thanked him, and then turned to say good-bye to her little sister. "Good-bye, my Joey. Take care of yourself."

"Good-bye, Madge. Have a good time!"

The porter lifted her down, for the train was actually beginning to move. She wriggled herself free of him, and turned to the other two. They at once responded. At the top of their voices they all yelled, "*Auf Wiedersehen*, Frau Doktor Russell!"

The last glimpse they had showed Madge's face nearly purple with embarrassment, while Jem was laughing so violently that he was holding on to the side of his seat.

"And that's the end of that," said Joey as they walked to the car to await the chaplain's arrival.

CHAPTER XXV

JOEY GETS THE SHOCK OF HER LIFE

"*AUF WIEDERSEHEN*, Frau Marani. It's been a gorgeous week, and we've enjoyed ourselves ever so!" Joey hugged kind Frau Marani with much good-will, and received a hearty kiss on either cheek.

"*Auf Wiedersehen, mein Kindchen!* We have enjoyed

having you. The dear God bless you and keep you safe always."

Herr Marani lifted the Robin up the steps and into the carriage then, and gently reminded his wife that the train would leave in a minute or two. "Go, my children," he said paternally. "Join Fraülein Juliet in the compartment, and let us see you safely there before we leave you."

They did as they were told. As Joey said, you generally *did* with Herr Marani. She could sometimes coax that good-natured giant, Herr Mensch, to recall his commands; but Herr Marani—never!

They were all three—Joey, Juliet, and the Robin—in the Southern express, bound for Belsornia, where Madge and Jem were waiting for them, and the Maranis had come down to Innsbruck to see them off. Gisela and Maria had not come, because Maria had caught cold the day before, and Gisela had stayed at home with her. They were going from Innsbruck to Verona, and from there they would get a train to Padua. At Padua they would be met by Captain Trevillion, who was to motor them to Firarto, in the heart of Belsornia. There *could* be no difficulty, for Vanna di Ricci's uncle, who lived in Verona, would put them into their train for Padua; so, as Madge had said in her letter to the three, they had nothing to do but sit still and let other people do the work.

Not that *they* took that literally! They had every intention of enjoying the journey, and they had felt quite annoyed when Herr Marani, spying a friend of his farther down the train, had asked him to look in on them from time to time. The friend, who had seven children of his own, had agreed with enthusiasm.

"Interfering giraffe!" was Joey's comment after they had left Innsbruck and were hurrying southwards through the Tyrol.

"*Joey!*" exclaimed Juliet as reprovingly as she could for smothering a giggle at Joey's choice of an epithet. Herr Melnarti was nearly as broad as he was long, so the comparison wasn't very apt.

"Well, he *is!*" retorted Joey.

However, she changed her mind presently. Herr Melnarti was a most delightful man, who adored children, and before long they were listening to his stories of Hans, and Meuda, and Friedel, and Klara, and Karl and Kâtchen, who were twins, and Gretel, the baby.

152

"They sound awfully nice," said Joey approvingly, when he had finished an account of how Friedal and Klara, who were *Junge Taugenichten* had dressed up the stump of an old tree in one of their sheets, and everyone had declared that the garden was haunted! Herr Melnarti laughed.

"I whipped Friedel for that," he said, "and then Klara cried, and said it was her fault as much as Friedel's, so I had to forgive them."

He was very good to them, and when night came he took the Robin into his arms and let her sleep there, as the elder girls were still wide awake. They would reach Verona early in the morning, and they had to spend the night in the train. When finally he rose to go, insisting that the other two should try to get some sleep too, he tucked them up in their rugs, and he came along to see that they were all right several times during the night. They were quite sorry to part with him when he left them in Signor di Ricci's care at Verona, and had promised them that he would tell his wife to send Klara to the Chalet School next term. As she duly arrived, and Kâtchen was promised for the following September, it may be gathered what *he* thought of *them!*

Signor di Ricci was "nice, but dull"—this was Juliet's verdict when they were telling their adventures at the palace. He gave them a good breakfast, and saw that they were in a carriage with pleasant people. Then he presented them each with a packet of chocolate, and said, *"A rivederci!"* and left them. At Padua they saw Captain Trevillion on the platform waving his hat to them, and then they were tucked into a splendid motor and set off on the last stage of their journey. It was very late when they arrived at Firarto, and they swept through wide silent streets, with mounted policemen here and there, and tall electric lamps.

The Robin slept through the whole of the arrival, and was undressed and put to bed all without awaking her, but Joey managed to open her eyes long enough to clutch her sister in a mighty hug and kiss her. Then she, too, went off to sleep once more, and was tucked up without so much as moving an eyelash. Juliet was properly awake, as became a young lady who was to become a college student in two months' time, and she ate the soup they brought her, and answered Mrs Russell's questions before she, too, sought her bed.

Then they all slept till the sun was shining brightly on the palace gardens, and Elisaveta had had her breakfast and was wandering anxiously up and down the long corridor, wishing they would hurry up and get dressed, for she had heaps to show them, and the afternoon would be completely taken up.

Joey woke up first, to meet her sister's eyes. She rolled over, and then sat up. "Hallo!" she exclaimed. "Whatever time is it?"

"Nearly ten," replied Madge, showing her watch.

Jo glanced at it casually, and then stared at her sister.

"What *is* the matter?" demanded Madge, thinking that she must have got a smudge on her face.

"You don't look a bit different," said Jo.

"May I ask *how* you expected me to look different?" demanded her sister.

"We-ell, I don't know. I thought you'd look—*married!*"

Madge coloured furiously. "Joey! You really are the edge! Of course I don't look different! To hear you, anyone would think I'd some idiotic disease!"

Joey grinned. "Not sure that it isn't! Oh, keep your hair on! I say, can I get up?"

"You'd better have breakfast first," decided Madge; "and here it comes."

Joey looked approvingly at the tray borne by a pretty girl in the Belsornian native dress. "It looks topping!" she remarked. "I'll wash my hands and face, if I may, and then I'll wire in! Where's the Robin?"

"Over there in the corner," replied her sister, waving her hand to a little bed in the opposite corner of the room. "Don't yell, Joey. I want her to have her sleep out. She was fearfully tired, poor baby!"

Joey lowered her voice obediently, but went on, "Where have they put Juliet?"

"Next door," returned Madge. "Elisaveta is on the other side of you, so you are all together. The schoolroom is beyond, and her own sitting-room is beyond that. She was showing it all to me yesterday. There are four huge bookcases, all full of books. Yes," as Joey's eyes grew bright, "you like that, I know; but do remember, Jo, that you are a visitor, and don't read *all* the time!"

Joey chuckled. "I won't! There are heaps of excursions to places where things happened—murders, and assassinations, and *oubliettes*, and things—and we are going to see them *all!*"

Madge laughed. "What a blood-thirsty collection! Yes, you may get up now if you have really finished your breakfast. The bathroom is over there, through that door. I have put out a clean white frock for you to wear this morning, and you must be careful not to tire yourself too much."

Joey looked up from the floor, where she was sitting putting on her bedroom slippers. "Why not?"

"Because—we are going to the city this afternoon, and you won't enjoy yourself if you aren't fresh."

Joey wasn't watching her, or she would have seen an indescribable expression on her sister's face as she said this. As it was, she trotted off to the bathroom and took her bath without troubling about the afternoon's expedition in the least; while Madge, after a look at the Robin, who still slept soundly, slipped away to see if Juliet had roused yet.

The morning was spent quietly in the garden, where Elisaveta showed her guests her own little plot, and the famous fountains, which were not playing that morning, and introduced them to various people as, "My chums from school."

Everyone was very nice to them, and everyone looked reverentially at Joey, much to her amazement. She couldn't imagine why they should all gape at her like that! After lunch, which they had in the King's private apartments, the children were sent to get ready for their drive.

"Venetta will come and help you, Juliet," said the Princess, "and Madame will dress the Robin, 'cos she said so. Alette is coming to you, Joey."

Joey opened eyes like saucers. "Why?" she demanded. "I can dress myself."

Elisaveta looked rather funny for a minute, and Jo was afraid she had hurt her friend's feelings; but before she could get out an apology Alette appeared on the scene and whisked her off.

"I can manage, honour bright!" Joey informed her.

Alette appeared to think not. She poured out hot water into the bowl while Joey was taking off her plain linen frock, and then told her to wash her hands and face. After that she examined the nails carefully and performed a little manicuring, after which she brushed Joey's hair till it shone like raw silk. Then she went to a cupboard and took from it a dainty little petticoat, all lace and muslin, and required her new charge to get into it.

Jo did as she was bidden; it seemed the easiest thing to do, but she wondered very much why all this fuss was necessary for a drive through the capital. However, she supposed it had to be done, and there didn't seem any use in arguing with Alette, who treated her as if she were no older than the Robin. When she was ready, the maid produced another white frock—but such a frock! Jo nearly gasped when she saw it. It was of white georgette, very simply made, and trimmed with cobwebby lace. Nothing could have been much plainer, for the lace only edged the neck and short sleeves, but it was exquisitely delicate, and she had never had one like it in her life. Alette slipped it over her head and adjusted it very carefully. Then she cast a glance at the dainty silk stockings and shoes which Joey had put on before she had washed; gave her hair a final touch with the brush, and then put on her head a big white hat with a twist of white silk round the crown. It was the simplest outfit, but Joey felt that she had never been so dressed as she was now.

"It will do, mademoiselle," said Alette, as she gave her a pair of long white gloves. "Put them on! So! Now that is all. His Majesty requests that you will go to the White Salon, and speak with him."

"But I don't know where it is," said Jo dismayedly.

"Venetta will have finished Mademoiselle Juliet," replied Alette, "and she will show you the way."

She opened the door as she spoke, and there was Venetta, a pretty rosy girl, who bobbed a curtsy as Jo appeared.

"Venetta, you will please take Mademoiselle Joey to the White Salon," directed Alette. "Then come back to me, as I shall need you."

Venetta bobbed another curtsy. "Will you follow me, miss," she said to Joey.

Jo meekly followed her along passages and down stairs to a great door, where two of the royal footmen promptly came to attention when they saw her.

"It is Mademoiselle Bettany," said Venetta.

The footmen saluted the startled child, and then flung back the doors, the older one announcing "Mademoiselle Bettany!" in tones which rang out.

"Mademoiselle Bettany" entered the great room, looking, as she felt, rather scared. The King, clad in a white uniform, with orders on his breast, and a glittering helmet, rose from a seat at the other end. Near him was Madge, looking prettier than ever in a white frock, too. Jem was standing behind her, wearing what Joey mentally termed "his gladdest rags," and the Crown Prince, in all the glory of his colonel's uniform, was on the other side of the King, who stretched out a hand to her.

"Josephine," he said gently, "I have asked you to come here so that my people may do honour to the girl who helped to save the Princess Elisaveta from the hands of Cosimo. The whole country knows what you did, and at what risk to yourself."

"But there wasn't any risk!" gasped Joey. "At least, not much—your Majesty."

"There was a terrible risk," replied the King. "Cosimo was mad, and what he might have done to you had he caught you, I shudder to think. It is the wish of my people and of the Government that we should show you how deeply grateful we all feel to you; so this afternoon you are to drive through the capital so that the people may see you, and then, at the Grand House—our Parliament House, you know—you are to be presented with a little remembrance of your courage."

Joey went white. What a horrible thing to happen. Perhaps the King understood, for he added gently, "You will do it, will you not? We hope to have Guides here in Belsornia, and the girls of Belsornia will like to see a Guide who has upheld her order so well."

"Yes, your Majesty," said Joey, looking up at him. "B—but I'd rather face Cosimo three times over, really!"

The King laughed kindly. "I am sure that you would. Never mind! It will soon be over, and you won't mind for the time it will take, will you?"

Joey said nothing, though she rather thought she *would*. Then the other three came in, all as beautifully dressed as she was, and they went out through two lines of footmen and entered the carriages. The King and the Crown Prince sat in the first, with Elisaveta and Joey facing them, and Madge and Jem came in the next, with Juliet and the Robin. After them followed the chief ministers of the Household, and then the Royal Household Troops fell in behind on their fine white horses, and the procession began. The streets were lined with people as they drove slowly through, and all the people were cheering.

157

"That is for you, Joey," said the Crown Prince. "Wave your hand to them, dear."

Joey did as she was told, and waved again and again, while the cheers thundered forth for the girl who had showed such courage and resource, and saved the Little Lady of Belsornia from what might have been a dreadful fate, for everyone knew now that Prince Cosimo had been insane, and not responsible for his actions.

At length they came to the Grand House, where they were received by the Ministers of the Crown, and Joey was led into a huge hall, where someone made a long speech, telling what she had done, and someone else followed with a longer. Then the King smiled at her, and she moved forward amidst more cheering and clapping, and the Prime Minister presented her with an illuminated address in a carved ivory casket.

Jo summoned her prettiest French to her aid. "Thank you so much," she said shyly. "It is so kind of you—but I couldn't have left the Princess without help, and I only did what anyone would have done."

There were more speeches, but she heard not a word of them, and then they were all back in the carriages and going through the streets again. When they finally reached the palace, Joey felt more tired than she had ever done in her life.

"Well done, Joey," said Prince Carol when they were all having tea—a sumptuous tea! "You did splendidly."

Joey fingered the string of pearls he and the King had given her when they had returned. "It's awfully kind of you, sir," she said, "but I'm glad I shan't have *that* to do any more! "

"You wouldn't like to be a princess, then?" asked the King.

Jo shook her head. "Oh *no!* I'm going to be an authoress!"

His Majesty smiled. "I hope you will. At the same time, when Elisaveta is older she will want a maid of honour, and I hope you will not refuse to accept the post when the time comes."

"If it doesn't interfere with my writing," replied Joey.

"It shan't," said Elisaveta. "But I'll want you, Joey, so you must promise."

"Oh well, if Madge says I may, then I will."

Madge looked at her with a smile. "I shall be very glad.

And I think," she added, "that we are all very glad that Princess Elisaveta came to the Chalet School."

Joey rose to her feet, her tea-cup in her hand. "Here's long life and good luck to Princess Elisaveta of the Chalet School!" she cried.

The Princess turned pink with pleasure. "It's me who ought to be glad that you have me," she said earnestly. "I'm *glad* to be Elisaveta of the Chalet School."